TARGET NINE

(THE SPY GAME–BOOK 9)

JACK MARS

Jack Mars

Jack Mars is the USA Today bestselling author of the LUKE STONE thriller series, which includes seven books. He is also the author of the new FORGING OF LUKE STONE prequel series, comprising six books; of the AGENT ZERO spy thriller series, comprising twelve books; of the TROY STARK thriller series, comprising seven books; of the SPY GAME thriller series, comprising ten books; of the JAKE MERCER thriller series, comprising five books (and counting); and of the new TYLER WOLF thriller series, comprising five books (and counting).

Jack loves to hear from you, so please feel free to visit www.Jackmarsauthor.com to join the email list, receive a free book, receive free giveaways, connect on Facebook and Twitter, and stay in touch!

ISBN: 978-1-0943-8544-0

BOOKS BY JACK MARS

TYLER WOLF THRILLER SERIES
DOUBLE AGENT (Book #1)
DOUBLE CROSS (Book #2)
DOUBLE ASSET (Book #3)
DOUBLE DOCTRINE (Book #4)
DOUBLE JEOPARDY (Book #5)

JAKE MERCER THRILLER SERIES
ABSOLUTE THREAT (Book #1)
ABSOLUTE DAMAGE (Book #2)
ABSOLUTE FORCE (Book #3)
ABSOLUTE PERIL (Book #4)
ABSOLUTE TREASON (Book #5)

THE SPY GAME
TARGET ONE (Book #1)
TARGET TWO (Book #2)
TARGET THREE (Book #3)
TARGET FOUR (Book #4)
TARGET FIVE (Book #5)
TARGET SIX (Book #6)
TARGET SEVEN (Book #7)
TARGET EIGHT (Book #8)
TARGET NINE (Book #9)
TARGET TEN (Book #10)

TROY STARK THRILLER SERIES
ROGUE FORCE (Book #1)
ROGUE COMMAND (Book #2)
ROGUE TARGET (Book #3)
ROGUE MISSION (Book #4)
ROGUE SHOT (Book #5)
ROGUE STRIKE (Book #6)
ROGUE ORDER (Book #7)

LUKE STONE THRILLER SERIES
ANY MEANS NECESSARY (Book #1)

OATH OF OFFICE (Book #2)
SITUATION ROOM (Book #3)
OPPOSE ANY FOE (Book #4)
PRESIDENT ELECT (Book #5)
OUR SACRED HONOR (Book #6)
HOUSE DIVIDED (Book #7)

FORGING OF LUKE STONE PREQUEL SERIES
PRIMARY TARGET (Book #1)
PRIMARY COMMAND (Book #2)
PRIMARY THREAT (Book #3)
PRIMARY GLORY (Book #4)
PRIMARY VALOR (Book #5)
PRIMARY DUTY (Book #6)

AN AGENT ZERO SPY THRILLER SERIES
AGENT ZERO (Book #1)
TARGET ZERO (Book #2)
HUNTING ZERO (Book #3)
TRAPPING ZERO (Book #4)
FILE ZERO (Book #5)
RECALL ZERO (Book #6)
ASSASSIN ZERO (Book #7)
DECOY ZERO (Book #8)
CHASING ZERO (Book #9)
VENGEANCE ZERO (Book #10)
ZERO ZERO (Book #11)
ABSOLUTE ZERO (Book #12)

PROLOGUE

The Himalayan Heritage Museum
Kathmandu, Nepal
9 a.m.

James and Emma Skinner smiled at each other as they passed through the front door of the museum, the first two people in the small line waiting for it to open. The brother and sister, both in their early twenties, had taken a year off after graduating to cross Asia together, and this moment was one they had both been looking forward to.

James always thought it funny how everyone commented on how close they were. Just a year apart, they'd been inseparable all through school and had all the same interests, especially Asian culture and hiking, which is why they had come to Nepal together. For the past month they'd hiked the Annapurna circuit and base camp routes, climbing high Himalayan passes and working their way up a long valley to the base camp, a stunning spot surrounded by snow-capped Himalayan peaks and a crackling glacial scree running beside it.

Now, footsore and more than a bit weary, they were back in Kathmandu seeing the sights.

Their first stop was the brand-new Himalayan Heritage Museum, opened just a few months before. It stood in the dusty modern outskirts of town, far away from the historic center, because the government didn't want to disturb the medieval squares and their countless temples and pagodas, many of which were being meticulously restored after the disastrous earthquake of 2015.

The museum, funded by the Nepali diaspora and UNESCO after the quake, aimed to bring together a vast collection of Himalayan artifacts not just from Nepal, but also Bhutan, Sikkim, and Tibet. In the outpouring of sympathy for the heritage and lives lost in the earthquake, museums and collectors around the world had donated rare items. The Nepali government had scoured their own museums for items as well to make the best collection of Himalayan artifacts anywhere.

James and Emma Skinner bought their tickets at the window and walked through the entrance of the grand concrete building, built to resemble a traditional pagoda but also designed by a top Japanese architect to be earthquake proof, climate controlled, and highly secure.

Once inside, they stopped and gasped.

The main entrance hallway was a masterpiece.

A huge golden statue of Garuda, the winged Hindu deity, faced an even more massive gold statue of four-armed Vishnu. Their serene eyes seemed to study each other while their minds had ascended to heaven.

On the walls hung silk tapestries from earlier centuries depicting scenes of religious ceremonies or the royal court. Framing the doorways on the three sides leading to other galleries were intricately carved wooden beams rescued from fallen temples.

James and Emma stood for a moment, soaking it all in.

Emma turned to her brother. “Let’s go check it out.”

She didn’t have to say what she meant. James knew she meant the Royal Vajra. The vajra had always been an important symbol for both of them ever since they started reading about Buddhism in high school, and the Royal Vajra, they knew, was unlike anything they had ever seen.

They headed through the righthand gallery, quickening their steps to outpace the steady trickle of early visitors coming through the entrance.

The brother and sister passed through an echoing chamber lined with golden buddhas, through another of elegant wooden carvings of Hindu deities, and found the room they sought.

The Royal Vajra sat in a glass case on a concrete podium the size of a large dinner table. They gasped as they beheld its beauty.

“Vajra” was the Sanskrit word for both “thunder” and “diamond.” A vajra was a pair of bulbs made up of five ribs connected at the center with a small handle. At the end of each bulb was a spike. It was the weapon of Indra, the Hindu king of heaven, and cut through ignorance and illusion like a sword cut through flesh. It also symbolized the male principle and would be used in rituals in conjunction with a bell, symbolizing the female principle.

But the Royal Vajra couldn’t be used that way, unless held by a giant. It was fully ten feet long.

No other vajra was that big. The ribs making the bulbs on either end were as thick as James’s arm, the space they contained big enough that

Emma could squeeze inside. The rod connecting the two bulbs was disproportionally thick.

Not only was the vajra enormous, but it was brilliantly preserved, the brass looking like it had been burnished yesterday.

This was a prize artifact of the Antiquities Authority of Nepal, held in storage at the royal palace for centuries before at last being displayed to the public here for the first time. As soon as James and Emma had read about it, they knew they'd have to come see it.

The brother and sister pressed their palms together in front of their heart. While not devout in either Hinduism or Buddhism, the main religions of this region, they respected many of their traditions and practiced meditation and yoga.

They stared at it, not speaking, barely even breathing.

James found he couldn't empty his mind as he had planned to in front of this sacred object. It was too stunning, too mysterious. Little was known about the thing or why it was so unusually large. The royal palace had no record of when they had acquired it, except that it had been acquired from the previous dynasty, the Gorka Kingdom, which had ruled from 1559 to 1768. Legend had it that one of the early Gorka rulers (no one was sure which) had found it in an ancient monastery on the Tibetan Plateau to the northeast and brought it back to Kathmandu. It was said to have incredible powers for enlightening the mind and had been a holy object venerated by centuries of Nepali kings.

Other than that, nothing was known about this unique artifact.

James stared, and wondered.

More people began to file in, both Nepalis and foreign tourists, all making a beeline for the Royal Vajra.

"Beautiful, isn't it?" a middle-aged Nepali man said in English and he took a place next to Emma. He, too, had his palms pressed together.

"It's amazing," Emma said breathlessly.

"They say it holds great power," the Nepali man said. "That it started normal size but gained so much power from the universe that it grew and grew until it became this size."

The American siblings stared at it with renewed interest. While they didn't actually believe that, the spiritual importance of this object wasn't lost on them.

James let out a long, slow breath and finally began to clear his mind.

Just as he settled into a meditative state, his sister doing the same at his side, a shot rang out.

James and Emma whirled around and heard shouting and screams in the next gallery.

Everyone froze. Was the museum being robbed?

The sound of heavy booted feet running in their direction made James's blood run cold.

Half a dozen masked men carrying AK-47s burst into the room. They shouted something in Nepali and all the Nepalis moved away from the Royal Vajra to the far wall, their hands in the air. James and Emma followed.

"No!" one of the masked men shouted in English. "Tourists to the other side!"

The tourists hurried to obey. James interposed himself between the gunmen and his sister. A thousand horrible scenarios passed through his imagination.

What if this was a terrorist group? Did Nepal have terrorist groups? He hadn't heard of any. But if this was a terrorist group, they might gun them all down. Or they might film them getting beheaded. Or they might take Emma and …

"Down on the floor!" the gunman shouted in English. A similar command was barked at the Nepalis. Everyone got down. James shielded Emma with his body.

If they come for her, I'll fight.

James wasn't sure how he'd fight. He had taken a couple of years of taekwondo in university, but he didn't think that would stand up to a gang of gun-toting maniacs.

Still, he'd fight. He'd rather die than see his sister hurt.

The gunman who spoke English walked over to the crowd of shivering tourists. Another walked over to the Nepalis.

Oh my God, they're going to kill us now.

Emma's hand slipped into his and they clasped.

For a moment, nothing happened. Then everyone heard the low hum of an engine.

A small forklift entered the gallery and drove up to the Royal Vajra.

A pair of gunmen riding it jumped off, wielding sledgehammers. They began to bang away at the safety glass, which slowly cracked and crumpled under the onslaught.

The two men facing the divided crowd began to speak.

"We are liberating the vajra for the people of the Himalayas," the one standing just a few feet away from James and Emma said in English. "It is wasted here as an object of curiosity for gawking tourists and ignorant Nepalis, just as is it was wasted when it was the private plaything of the king. Now it will be an object of power for the people!"

He raised his fist in the air.

The two masked men with the sledgehammers cleared away the last of the glass, hopped back on the forklift, and moved it forward.

The arms slid under the two club ends of the Royal Vajra, moved upwards, and lifted the sacred object.

Beep. Beep. Beep.

The forklift backed up.

Several of the Nepalis cried out and rose. One of the gunmen let loose with his AK-47, stitching a line of bullet holes into the wall above their heads.

They all dove back down to the floor.

The forklift backed out of the gallery, turned, and sped off toward the entrance hall.

"Power to the people of the Himalayas!" shouted the man in front of them, raising his fist to the air once more.

He and the others ran out of the gallery, leaving the trembling visitors to stare at the empty plinth where once sat Nepal's most sacred object.

CHAPTER ONE

Dublin, Ireland
That evening

Jacob Snow felt like a tourist.

Of course, that was the point since he was pretending to be a tourist, but it still felt low-key embarrassing.

He was sidling up to the bar at the Lucky Shamrock, a pub in the historic center of Dublin. The Lucky Shamrock featured nightly live Irish music, Guinness on tap, and virtually no Irish people among its clientele. It was a tourist place, plain and simple, with a tourist crowd and tourist prices.

The kind of place the guidebooks all called "authentic."

Jacob found the whole scene cringy, especially the drunk Americans faking Irish accents and the even drunker American trying to do a jig in front of the band.

"Two pints of Guinness, please," Jacob said.

The bartender had already started pouring one Guinness when Jacob appeared at the bar. He grabbed a second pint glass. The number was the only thing that varied among customer requests, not the product.

Everyone here drank Guinness.

Once he got his pints and paid the extortionate price, he turned from the bar and scanned the cramped interior with its oak beams and wooden floor. Faded prints hung on the walls. The pub dated to the eighteenth century, if you could believe the website, a respectable but not venerable age for an Irish pub.

He walked back to the small round table where Jana sat. She, too, was scanning the crowd. She gave an almost imperceptible shake of the head as he sat down.

No, their target hadn't arrived yet.

"Sláinte," he said, raising his glass.

"Is that how you say cheers in Gaelic?" Jana asked.

"Who knows?"

“There’s a pronunciation guide on the back of the menu,” she said, flipping it over. It was wet with someone else’s spilled beer.

“Do you believe it?”

“No more than I believe the potted history written on here.”

“Ah yes, always critical of source material. Anyway, sláinte.”

They drank.

"Hmm, this is good, at least," Jana said. Suddenly, she looked down at the menu and lowered her voice. "At the door."

Jacob turned to toast the Irish band, pretending to be drunk. He even sloshed a bit of his beer onto the already-soaked floor.

It was a good skill, pretending to be drunk. Very useful when on recon.

The movement allowed him to catch the entrance out of the corner of his eye.

Paddy O’Neil had just walked in.

Yes, there really were Irishmen named Paddy, and this particular Paddy was what the English would call “a rough bit of work.”

He was the second-in-command of the Modern Republican Army, a continuation of the Irish Republican Army that had laid down its arms and agreed to peace talks. The Modern Republican Army wanted to continue the armed struggle against the United Kingdom and unite Ireland by force, but unlike other dissident Republican splinter groups that rejected the Northern Ireland peace process, the Modern Republican Army rejected the Marxist ideology of its predecessors, had a slick online presence, and advocated for a “truly united Ireland” by inviting Protestants into its ranks.

Not that it got any takers.

A lot of people in the CIA and MI5 had snickered at the Modern Republican Army for being ridiculously out of touch. They stopped snickering when the MRA set off a bomb in a Belfast police station that killed five police officers and a little old lady walking her dog on the street outside.

Further attacks followed, and the MI5 began to pay attention. The CIA got brought in when the British discovered that much of the MRA’s funding came from producing methamphetamine and shipping it over to the U.S. for sale.

Which is why Jacob and Jana were called in.

After their last operation and the revelation that the shadowy organization known as the Antiquities Division knew where they lived, the CIA had moved them to a safehouse in the Irish countryside, a lovely little stone cabin surrounded by rolling hills, sheep, and solitude.

That solitude got disturbed when the MRA reared its ugly head and the CIA asked them to do a simple surveillance job.

Them, not just Jacob. He was still shaking his head about that one. Jana had jumped onto so many CIA missions that they just assumed she'd want to go along.

She did. Jacob, not so much. He liked the sheep and the solitude.

But here he was, and here was Paddy O'Neil.

Like many terrorist leaders, Paddy did not live in the county he terrorized. His attacks were all in Northern Ireland while he lived in the Republic of Ireland. That's where the meth operation was. The bombings were all in the north.

Paddy was here at the Lucky Shamrock to find a new cook for his meth after his last one had a little traffic accident courtesy of the CIA. Paddy didn't know his cook had been driving sober, and the crash wasn't his fault. He also didn't know that the lean, unkempt man sitting in the back room waiting to meet him wasn't a meth cook, but an Irish MI5 operative.

Paddy grabbed a Guinness at the bar, looked around at the scene with obvious distaste, and headed for the back room.

The MRA second-in-command had requested that the meetup be in the Lucky Shamrock, figuring there would be fewer eyes on them. No self-respecting Irishman went to the Lucky Shamrock. Even the band and the bartender had that glassy-eyed look that showed they were mentally elsewhere.

Paddy passed right by Jacob and Jana, both in their "kiss me I'm Irish" t-shirts that marked them out as anything but, and walked into the back room.

The back room was tiny, with a single table already taken up by the MI5 agent. Jacob could see through the open doorway. Paddy sat down next to him. Not opposite him. Paddy was the kind of guy who always had his back to the wall and his eyes on the door.

They greeted one another. Jacob couldn't hear a word over the sound of the music and the drunken bawling of the drinkers. Paddy had picked his spot well.

Then the MRA terrorist pulled out what looked like a cell phone but Jacob immediately recognized as what they affectionately called in the business a "sniffer". It could tell if the MI5 guy was wearing a wire. Paddy was quite the techie.

The MI5 agent sipped his beer with unfeigned calm. He wasn't wearing a wire. He didn't need to. Jana's phone, set on the table in front of her, was also not a phone. It was a highly directional listening device that blanked out the ambient noise and picked up the sounds of whatever it was pointed at.

It was pointed at the back table and was recording everything.

Paddy O'Neil and the MI5 guy started to chat. Jacob talked to Jana about nothing in particular to have an excuse to face their direction. Jana did a good job of not looking over her shoulder. The temptation was big on a surveillance job like this, and a lot of rookie agents got too curious. Not Jana. She just chatted away about the artifacts they'd seen in the national museum like she would have if they really were on vacation. She was a natural.

Too natural.

When he had first met her, Jana Peters hadn't wanted anything to do with the CIA. She hated the organization because her father, his mentor Aaron Peters, had spent most of her childhood and adolescence far away from her on secret missions. But circumstances had thrown her into it and not only had she survived (a miracle in and of itself) but had thrived. Soon, she was sneaking along after him. Then, the CIA caved in and let her come along unofficially. Now, it was semiofficial. There seemed no stopping her. She actually got a thrill from it all.

He didn't. He was sick of the whole damn thing. The problem was, the world was an evil, dangerous place and he was one of the best people to keep it safe.

And that wasn't arrogance. Some people accused him of arrogance, of course. None of those people had saved the world half a dozen times.

Jana never called him arrogant. Immature, annoying, and uncultured, but never arrogant.

So they sat there pretending to be tourists, not having to pretend being in love, while Jana's listening device recorded Paddy's entire conversation with the MI5 agent.

The agent slapped the table and gave Paddy a thumbs up, a signal that the deal had been made. The two talked for another minute, shook hands, and then Paddy rose. Jacob and Jana kissed. It seemed like the natural thing to do and kept them from the temptation of looking at him as the terrorist left.

At least that was the plan.

Instead, something else happened, because something else always happened on these missions.

Two drunk American tourists detached themselves from the crowd. One ran for Jacob and Jana's table and picked up the listening device. The other went for the MI5 agent, pulling out a gun.

Then several things happened at once.

The MI5 agent threw his pint glass at the gunman's face. As the glass smashed on the man's forehead, the gun went off.

At the same moment, Jacob threw his own pint in the face of the man who had grabbed the listening device.

And Paddy, of course, drew a gun.

Why is nothing straightforward in my life? Jacob asked himself.

Things went downhill from there.

CHAPTER TWO

Jana Peters reacted on the instinct born of long training sessions with her father and her more recent practice as a kickboxer.

As the man who had grabbed her listening device wiped the beer from his eyes, Jana put her hands on the bottom of the table, rose, and pushed it at him. The force of impact was enough for it to make him stagger backwards, hitting Paddy and taking off his aim enough for his first bullet to embed itself in the back of Jacob's chair instead of his chest.

Jana kept pushing on the table, but the smooth wood, made slick by beer and God-knows-what else, slipped from her grasp and fell hard on her foot.

She was left facing two very angry Irish terrorists, one still holding her listening device, the other still holding a compact automatic pistol.

Paddy was out of reach, so she threw a right cross at the man who had grabbed her listening device.

It caught him on the cheekbone, whipping his head to the side. She had hoped it would knock him back against Paddy and throw off his aim again.

It didn't.

Paddy took a step to the side to get a clear shot and aimed right at her …

… only to get knocked to the side as Jacob hit him with the power of a locomotive.

Both men went down, Jacob gripping his gun hard and pushing it away from both of them. It went off again and Jana thought she heard someone cry out. Hard to tell since the whole pub was shouting now.

Jana extracted her foot from beneath the table, glanced at the MI5 agent to see had disarmed but was still struggling with the bloody-faced terrorist who had come for him, and turned back to face her closest opponent.

Despite the beer to the face, followed by a hard fist, the man had recovered himself enough to pocket her listening device, block her uppercut, and throw a haymaker that nearly decapitated her.

Jana backed up.

"Never get distracted in a fight," her father always used to tell her. *"Don't look at what your comrades are doing when you have your own problem right in front of you."*

I should have listened.

Glancing at the MI5 agent, who was doing just fine, had made her lose her advantage.

As Jacob and Paddy struggled on the floor (*you're getting distracted again!*) the man sidestepped the table and came at her.

Jana's back was to the wall, and she had little room to maneuver, so she advanced. Blocking a right cross that sent a shockwave of pain up her left arm, she gave him a right hook that he ducked like the trained boxer he was turning out to be. Only now did Jana notice the cauliflower ears, the flattened nose, and numerous facial scars.

Great. Just great.

He swung again, Jana ducked to save her arm, and then had to block a left jab that sent another pulse of pain through her body. This guy's punches felt like sledgehammers. She sure didn't want to take one to the face.

Jana ducked to the right, getting more space between them. He followed, and Jana retreated another step and lashed out with her leg, smacking him on the side of the knee.

That slowed him but didn't stop him.

She dodged his next swing, kicked at his leg again, and kept circling, looking for an advantage.

The quickest way to end this fight would be to punch him in the throat, but he kept his chin down like all experienced fighters. The next quickest way would be to kick him in the balls, but he kept his body at an angle, even more so now that he knew she could kick with force and accuracy.

It looked like there would be no easy way to beat this guy.

He swung again, Jana dodged again and landed a quick jab that achieved nothing. When he advanced once more, she gave him a combo leg kick left cross that staggered him, but when she dove in for a decisive blow got a fist in her ribs that made her gasp.

She just managed to duck the next swing, took the follow up on her shoulder, and backpedaled as quick as she could. He came in, eyes gleaming, eager for the kill.

And that's when Jana got him. He came in too fast, overestimating the damage he had done. Jana kicked him in the ankle, timing it perfectly when all the weight was on it. He fell over and landed hard on the wooden floor.

A well-placed kick slammed his head into the floor. His whole body shook, stunned by the blow. Jana kicked him again, then a third time so he'd stop moving.

Only then did Jana look around to see Jacob had pummeled Paddy into submission, the MI5 agent had done the same with his opponent, and a tourist sat on the ground, holding his bloody ankle.

The stray shot. Damn, it hit an innocent bystander.

All too often, these missions got messy. How many innocent people had died in the course of saving more lives?

A couple of women were helping the wounded civilian and the bartender had brought out a first aid kit. He was on the phone, no doubt calling the police and an ambulance. The rest of the pub had cleared out.

The MI5 man strolled up to the bartender and flashed a badge. The bartender went pale, then a flicker of rage passed over his features. An Irishman working for the UK's interior spy service was not welcome even in a tourist trap like the Lucky Shamrock.

Jana tensed, waiting to see if the bartender would strike.

He glanced around at the three agents standing in the room, and the three big men sprawled on the floor, and thought the better of it.

Jacob turned to the MI5 man. "You didn't tell me he'd have backup."

"If I knew, I would have told you. And you heard them talking like the rest. They're either Yanks like you or the most convincing voice actors in Dublin."

"This means there's more of an American connection than we thought," Jana said.

"We'll find out more once we get them to the station," the MI5 agent said. He turned to the two women applying first aid. "Hey, when you're done with that first aid kit, let me have it. I gave that Yank terrorist a proper glassing."

"I love that 'glass' is a verb in this country," Jacob said with a grin.

Sirens wailed in the distance, signaling the imperfect end to what should have been a routine mission.

***

Later that evening, after a long debriefing session and an hour's drive to their cottage, Jana leaned against Jacob on a sofa in front of a crackling fire. The wood beams and stone walls of their old cottage caught the flickering light and cast it back as a warm glow. Jana snuggled a little closer to her lover and sighed.

"I'm glad that guy only got grazed," she said. "Still, I feel a bit bad."

"Don't. It was Paddy's fault for drawing a gun in a crowded pub, not your fault for stopping him from killing anyone."

"Still … "

"No." Jacob ended that line of thought with a kiss.

"I guess it's mission accomplished, though. We got Paddy O'Neil and two American operatives. Even if they don't talk, we've seriously hurt their operation."

"Another win for the good guys," Jacob said, squeezing her.

"And girls."

"Oh, yes."

They were still supposed to be on R and R. The Dublin embassy had requested their help, however, because the only CIA operative assigned to the Republic of Ireland was busy on another mission.

Western Europe had become low priority lately thanks to all the troubles in the Middle East, and thus had become seriously undermanned. Jana had a sneaking suspicion that was why their new safehouse was over here instead of another spot in the United States.

Tricky.

Jana had always hated the CIA for its lies its, collateral damage, and the fact that it had taken her father away for much of her life. Indeed, the CIA had led her to believe he had been killed in action. Even Jacob had been fooled.

Despite this, she had warmed up to the CIA in the past year after a string of missions that had her circling the globe and stopping several threats to world security. That had made her realize just how important its work was.

Even so, she hadn't been fooled. It was still a manipulative branch of government with its own agenda, power plays, and willingness to sacrifice its operatives for the "greater good."

The CIA was very far from perfect.

And yet it had given her a life she never thought she wanted, and an importance she never thought she could achieve.

It had also given Jana her father back, and given her the man she loved.

The CIA was a mixed bag and always would be.

At least now maybe the CIA would leave them in peace for a while.

The ringing of Jacob's encrypted satellite phone in the next room told her otherwise.

Jana groaned. Jacob looked even less happy. He paused. The ringing continued, echoing through the quiet and once-peaceful country cottage.

With a curse, Jacob leapt up and went to answer it.

CHAPTER THREE

"Yes, sir?" Jacob said as he picked up the phone, trying to keep the irritation out of his tone.

Tyler Wallace's voice came on the other end. While he was Jacob's station chief back home and technically not in command of him here, the higher-ups in the Company had decided they worked so well together that he remained his direct commander.

"I heard about tonight's operation. Congratulations on getting O'Neil and his two guards."

"Those two guards were a surprise," Jacob said. "They blended with the crowd perfectly. And they spotted the listening device somehow. Probably when Jana switched it on."

"Don't beat yourself up about it. Mission accomplished, and from what I hear that tourist will make a full recovery."

"Jana will be glad to hear it."

A moment's silence.

Here it comes.

"Are you feeling fit, Agent Snow?"

Does it matter?

"What's threatening the world now?"

Jacob wasn't able to keep the irritation out of his voice this time. A couple of months ago, he had been planning on quitting. He had written and rewritten his resignation letter over and over in his head. But before he could put pen to paper, he'd been called on another mission, another chance to save the world.

He wished he wasn't so good at it. Then he could quit with a clean conscience.

"There are always threats, Agent Snow. You know that. The question is, are you feeling fit?"

"Yes, I suppose I'm feeling fit," Jacob grumbled. "Jana's feeling fit too."

She'll leap on any mission you offer her. I wish to hell she wouldn't.

"There's a problem in Nepal."

"Nepal? That's not even close to my area of expertise."

"I'm aware of that, but we suspect Chinese involvement and too many of our operatives are suspected by the Chinese. We need a fresh face."

"You mean two fresh faces."

"Well, yes. This mission has an archaeological angle Ms. Peters would be highly suitable for."

Jacob sighed, rubbed his eyes, and said, "Let me get her in here and put you on speaker."

"All right."

He turned to call to her and found her standing at the door.

Jesus Christ.

He grimaced, motioned her over, and put Wallace on speaker.

"Hello, Ms. Peters. Glad to have you on board. Are you familiar with the Royal Nepalese vajra?"

Jana blinked. "Um, vaguely."

Jacob was surprised. It was rare that Jana blanked on a cultural question.

"But you have heard of it."

"Yes, it's a giant Buddhist ritual object that's been in the Nepalese royal family for years. Why?"

"It was stolen from the Himalayan Heritage Museum yesterday."

"Oh. Do you think Professor Colin Harlow took it?"

Professor Harlow and his team of militants had blown up a series of hydroelectric dams a few months before in order to destroy hidden chambers within them containing a treasury of ancient artifacts. These chambers had been built by the Antiquities Division, a secret branch of the U.S. government formed after World War Two in order to hide and study these artifacts. The Division believed they were evidence of a lost civilization that had developed high technology before it destroyed itself and the remains got erased by the last Ice Age.

Jacob found it believable. Jana, he knew, remained unconvinced.

"We don't know," Wallace said. "We actually suspect Chinese involvement. A group of heavily armed masked men overpowered the guards, killing one, and rushed in with a forklift. They separated the Nepalese from the tourists, and each group got a harangue in their own language. Nepalese witnesses said the gunmen spoke Nepali to them and to each other like native speakers. Both groups got basically identical statements that the vajra was being liberated for the people of Nepal and that it didn't belong to the royal family."

Jacob leaned forward. "For the people? They used that term?"

"A couple of times. And they raised their left fist in the air."

"Sounds like Communists. Isn't there a Communist guerrilla group in Nepal?"

"There is. It's called the Nepalese People's Liberation Front, and they've been increasing their activity lately. It's been mostly confined to raiding isolated police stations and extorting villagers in the rural east, especially in the mountainous region near the Chinese border."

"Are they supported by China?" Jana asked.

"Yes. They receive training within China and armaments. This has caused tensions with India, which sees any Chinese threat to Nepal as a threat to itself. New Delhi sees Nepal as a buffer zone and doesn't take lightly to any incursions there. They've said if the situation gets worse, they might be forced to move troops into Nepal."

"What do the Nepalese think of this?" Jacob asked.

"They'd see it as a violation of their sovereignty. They have always feared Indian domination more than Chinese domination. The border with China is the Himalayan mountains. All they have to do is guard a few high mountain passes. The border with India is open lowlands. Indian tanks could roll into Kathmandu in a few hours."

"And what's the U.S. stance?" Jana asked.

"The U.S. is stuck in a bind. India is an important ally and an important trading partner. China is a rival and an even more important trading partner. Nepal isn't important geopolitically, but public sympathy generally goes to the underdog in situations like this. To make matters more complicated, China has always denied funding the Nepali People's Liberation Front and we don't actually have any solid proof that they are, at least nothing we can share with the world that wouldn't compromise some of our operatives."

Jacob nodded. This was a common problem. You gathered intelligence but the specificity of that intelligence, if revealed, would point a finger at the agent. Photos from inside a military base, for example, or copies of secret memos only a few have access to.

"How big of an impact is having this … what's it called?"

"Vajra," Wallace and Jana said at the same time.

"How big of an impact is having this vajra thing stolen going to be?"

"Pretty major for south and southeast Asia. It's one of the holiest Buddhist relics and it has only been put on public display in the past couple of months. It's the private property of the Nepalese royal family and used to be locked up in their palace. There's going to be a tough response. Already the Nepalese army is gearing up for a major offensive on the Communist rebels. This could destabilize the entire region."

"Have the Nepalese People's Liberation Front made any demands?"

"None."

"Have they taken responsibility?"

"There hasn't been a peep from them. Not a statement, no negotiator under a white flag. Nothing."

"Huh. That doesn't make sense."

"No, it doesn't."

"But why us? I mean, neither of us speaks Nepali or Chinese, and Jana isn't an expert on this stuff."

"As I said, we need fresh faces, and you guys have been batting a thousand. But I don't want you going if you're unwilling. The Company owes you enough R and R to last you until you're using walkers. So if you want to bow out, I won't judge you."

Jacob looked at Jana … and despaired. She had that eager gleam in her eye that he knew so well. She wanted to do it.

And he didn't. He was thoroughly sick of the whole game. He wasn't even qualified for this stuff. He was no expert in the Far East. It was a totally different region with totally different rules.

When you didn't understand the rules, those rules could bury you.

CHAPTER FOUR

It took a full day to fly from Dublin to Berlin and then take a direct flight to Kathmandu, and by the time they got to Nepal's capital city, Jana was jetlagged and impatient.

The jetlag she could shrug off. She certainly had experienced enough of that in her life.

The impatience was a little more difficult. It had taken so long to get to the other side of the world, and the trail might be going cold.

This was confirmed when the local CIA operative and a local police detective met them at the airport.

The CIA operative, a husky Nepalese-American with a disarming Southern drawl, shook their hand as they collected their luggage.

"I'm Agent Arjun Tamang. Pleased you could help us on this. My colleague here is Detective Ram Gurung of the Kathmandu police."

"Pleased to meet you," Detective Gurung said in careful but correct English. "I hope you had a good flight."

"We did, thank you," Jana replied. "We're anxious to get started."

"Your hotel has already been arranged," the detective said and motioned to a police officer standing nearby. "My assistant will take your luggage to your rooms. Would you like to see the museum immediately?"

"I think that would be best," Jacob said. "Any leads?"

"The gunmen got away," the CIA operative said, "but they left behind an interesting clue at the museum. I think it's best that you see it for yourself."

The two men led them to the parking lot and Detective Gurung got in the driver's seat of an unmarked car. They passed through unremarkable suburbs of concrete buildings dotted with a few fields. It looked like any other city in the developing world, except the people looked anxious. She even saw a woman crying on a street corner. On another corner, a crowd had gathered for a protest, with the police trying to calm them down.

They passed the protest by and continued down a street lined with concrete buildings and shops. While Jana had never been to Nepal, she had heard the more picturesque parts were in Kathmandu's historic center or out in the villages. In the far dusty distance, she could just make out the snow-capped peaks of the Himalayas.

Her heart thrilled a little. While she had always been more of a desert person than a mountain person, she had loved her hikes in the Atlas range in Morocco, and hoped this trip took them closer to the world's largest mountain range.

She reminded herself that this was no pleasure trip. If they went into the Himalayas, it would probably be to seek out one of the bases for the Nepalese People's Liberation Front.

As if reading her thoughts, Jacob asked, "Do you have equipment for us?"

"That's not a problem," Agent Arjun Tamang replied. "We'll fit you out tonight after we see the museum."

"You are here as guests," Detective Ram Gurung added. "You will have all that you need. It is uninvited guests that we need to watch out for."

"Still no statement from the Nepalese People's Liberation Front?"

"They are unusually silent," the police detective replied with a frown as he steered between trucks and motorcycles on the busy road. "They always make a comment on any major event because they want to be part of the conversation. The fact that they haven't commented on the largest theft in our nation's history is significant."

"Significant how?" Jana asked.

The detective shrugged. "We're not sure yet. But the Communists have no religion. They're crazy people with no morals. They're up to no good, I am sure of it."

They came to a large pagoda-shaped concrete building that Jana recognized as the Himalayan Heritage Museum, set in a suburb in the middle of a large park with grass and trees.

That park, and the museum itself, were empty of visitors. A police cordon had been set up around the building and park. In addition to the police, there were a good number of soldiers too, as well as a pair of armored personnel carriers with heavy machine guns mounted on top.

"If only we had this much security two days ago," the detective said with a sigh. He produced his badge at the roadblock and spoke a few words of Nepali to the soldiers and police officers there. The men, all toting automatic weapons, stared at the foreigners curiously for a moment and then waved them through.

Detective Gurung parked in front of the museum's front steps and led them inside.

Jana only a had a moment to marvel at the art treasures all around her before they we led to a back gallery where the Royal Vajra had been kept.

A large plinth stood in the center, the safety glass lying in a thousand pieces all around it. Both of the Nepalese men fell silent for a moment, their faces grim.

"This was a terrible thing," Detective Gurung whispered. "A terrible thing."

"We've already seen the security footage on the plane ride over," Jacob said. "It looked like a professional operation."

The CIA operative nodded. "Well planned. This is what we wanted to show you."

He pointed to a symbol spray painted in yellow paint on the wall to the right, directly under a text about the Royal Vajra.

It was an odd symbol that Jana didn't recognize but right away suspected was related to the vajra symbol.

It appeared to be three lightning bolts tied at the center and radiating out on either side, or perhaps six lightning bolts tied end to end. Thus, is had a similar shape to the vajra and perhaps a similar meaning. One of the meanings of "vajra" was thunder, and lightning was associated with thunder. She'd taken a crash course on Buddhism on the trip over.

"I'm not terribly familiar with Buddhist and Hindu symbolism," Jana said. "What's the significance of this?"

"We don't know. None of us had ever seen this before."

The two Nepalese looked at her as if they had been hoping she'd have an answer.

The detective added, "We have arranged for you to speak to a professor at the university. Perhaps he can help."

"Any trace of the gunmen?" Jacob asked.

"They drove out of Kathmandu, heading north. After about fifty miles, they ditched the forklift, the truck that had carried it, and two vans that had carried the bulk of the gunmen. All were torched. The forklift was found outside the truck so obviously they used it to transfer the Royal Vajra to another vehicle. While the vehicles were all too badly burned to get fingerprints or DNA evidence, we did get some serial numbers. All were from vehicles reported stolen in various places in northern India in the past year."

"They planned this well."

The detective nodded. "Yes. We are wondering if those vehicles might have been supplied by the Indian government, that the leftist slogans the gunmen shouted were just a ruse. Or perhaps they paid the Communists to do it. Perhaps India is making an excuse to intervene. Their own Gulf of Tonkin incident."

The Nepalese-American CIA operative raised a cautioning hand. "We shouldn't jump to conclusions. As you told me yourself, most of the stolen vehicles recovered in Nepal have their origin in India."

The detective snorted and muttered something in Nepali.

"Does the government have any contact people who can get in touch with the Nepalese People's Liberation Front?" Jacob asked.

"A couple," the detective said. "One can't be found. The other said he has to go through a second contact and claims he can't get in touch."

"And who are these people?"

"I'm not authorized to reveal their identities. It's very delicate. But believe me when I say that they are reliable go-betweens. For whatever reason, the Communists don't want to speak to anyone."

"Odd that they'd neither confirm nor deny their involvement," Jana said.

The others nodded but had nothing to add.

"I don't think we'll learn much more here," Jana said. "Let's go see this professor."

***

Professor Mahesh Bishwakarma had a corner office in an old wooden building on the campus of the University of Nepal. Like the city it was in, it was a mixture of old and new. The core campus consisted of half a dozen wooden buildings with pagoda-style eaves marking each floor arranged around a central garden. The newer and larger campus was made up of utilitarian concrete buildings.

Professor Bishwakarma was a sloppily dressed man who needed a haircut and someone to organize his office. Bookshelves were crammed with volumes. The desk and a couple of the chairs were piled high with papers. Academics were more or less the same the world over.

Like their minders, the professor spoke good English. After introductions, the detective showed him the photo of the strange lightning symbol spray painted in the room.

His reaction was as electric as the lightning it appeared to represent.

He said something in Nepali, rapid and lengthy. The detective cut him off in English.

"Remember our guests, professor."

"Oh, right. So sorry." He adjusted his glasses. "This is a *car mey.*"

"What does that translate to?" Jana asked.

"That's a matter of debate. It's from an early precursor to all the Sino-Tibetan languages called Proto-Sino-Tibetan that evolved around 4,000 years ago. Some say it's much older."

"I see," she said, more to be agreeable than accurate. Jana was getting well out of her specialty here.

"The language is not very well understood since there are no written records. Instead, we trace back through living and historical languages to find common root words."

Jana nodded. This was common practice in historical linguistics.

"The significance of the construction *car mey* is not fully understood, although it seemed to be an antecedent of words in Nepali, Tibetan, and Dzongkha, the language of Bhutan. Literally the translation is 'sun fire', but the construction seems to have the meaning of 'power', but more like energy than political power or strength."

"Spiritual energy?"

"Some scholars think so. Others, myself included, think it's more like the energy of an adrenaline rush or the force of a mountain stream."

"I see. And what would it mean in this context?"

"Unclear. Perhaps the thieves believed the symbol referred to spiritual power."

"Why do you think this is incorrect?"

Professor Bishwakarma smiled. "To explain this would take several days, just like you explaining to me the seriation of Late Roman pottery in the ancient province of Mauritania."

Jana laughed. "We do get rather specialized, don't we?" Then, more seriously, she observed, "You were quite taken aback when you saw the symbol. Why?"

"Because it came up recently. A year ago, a colleague of mine who was conducting a survey of the caves along the border between Nepal and Chinese-controlled Tibet found numerous examples of cave art with many strange symbols he couldn't decipher. He showed me some of them. One of the most common was this very symbol."

Jana blinked. "And how old was this cave art?"

"Quite old. These were well-preserved caves high in the Himalayas, where the low temperatures and lack of flora and fauna kept the cave environment in near stasis. He hadn't dated them thoroughly, but he thought they had to be tens of thousands of years old. He was preparing his findings for publication when he disappeared."

"He disappeared?"

The detective cut in. "Are you referring to Professor Suresh Joshi?"

"Yes."

"I'm familiar with that case. He disappeared almost a year ago. His wife phoned the police when he didn't come home from work. His car was discovered in a park on the outskirts of town. No trace of him was ever found. He hadn't made any large withdrawals from the bank, there was no evidence he was having an affair or had made any enemies, and he wasn't a drinker or drug user."

"Suicide?" Jacob suggested.

The professor shook his head. "He was not suicidal. He was a happy family man about to publish the discovery of his career."

Jana felt a strange tingling. She had seen other caves with strange ancient drawings, and even stranger interpretations.

The last mission took them to northern India, where Robert Bledshaw of the Antiquities Division had shown them cave paintings that were thousands of years old and seemed to show hovercraft and rockets as well as images of bacteria as seen through a microscope.

Impossible, and yet she hadn't been able to fully explain them away.

"Where is the documentation for his findings?" she asked.

"Professor Joshi always kept all his files in his briefcase. He was very protective of them, fearing that someone might steal his findings. We were old friends and I was the only one he confided with. That briefcase went missing along with himself."

"He must have had some people on his team. Graduate students or something."

"He had one graduate student who died in a trekking accident last autumn. Everyone else on the team were local Sherpas. I don't know how to get in touch with them. I don't even know their names."

This was beginning to sound suspicious. Really, really suspicious.

Jana looked over at Jacob and saw he was thinking the same thing.

"Could we speak to his wife?" Jana asked. "I think we'd like to delve into this a bit more."

CHAPTER FIVE

Jana sat with Jacob and their two local assistants in the small but colorfully decorated living room of an apartment in a middle-class district of Kathmandu.

Heena Joshi, wife and presumed widow of Professor Suresh Joshi, sat in a chair opposite them. She looked sad and very, very tired. On the walls in between colorful textiles hung photos of her family—herself, the vanished husband, and three smiling children.

Jana felt a lump in her throat when she realized those children hadn't smiled for many months.

Through the detective's translation, Heena said, "I don't know what else I can tell you. I've told the police everything many times."

Jana put a hand on hers. "I'm an archaeologist like your husband. I think that what he discovered might have something to do with his disappearance."

"Why would someone kidnap him for that? They were just old paintings in a cave."

"That's what we're trying to determine. Has anyone reached out to you to ask about your husband's findings? Anyone not associated with his university? Anyone you don't know?"

Heena thought for a moment. "Many people came right after he was … he disappeared … " *Poor woman,* Jana thought. *She almost said 'murdered'* " … but they were all friends or colleagues. But now that you ask, there was one man, a strange fellow. His name was Prakash. He said he knew my husband, but I had never met him before. He did know all about his investigations. I was surprised. He wasn't an archaeologist. He owns a tourist shop near Durbar Square. He was most anxious to see my husband's notes. I told him that they had vanished with him and he looked very disappointed. I never heard from him again."

"You said he was strange. How?"

"Wild eyed. Very eager. I don't know what it's like for American archaeologists, but here in Asia, they attract a lot of crazy people with crazy theories. Prakash struck me as one of those. I didn't talk to him for long, and I never heard from him again. He left his card saying to get in touch if I ever heard from my husband or found his notes. I think I have it somewhere."

She went into a back room. After a long search, she returned with a cheaply printed business card that read, “Prakash Rai, Antiques Merchant, 5 Gangalal Marg, Kathmandu.”

Jana turned to the others. “I think we should check him out.”

***

Gangalal Marg was a short street not far from Durbar Square, the most famous historic square in the city. As they crossed it, Jana marveled at the large building of red stone to one side with elaborately carved wooden windows and a soaring multi-tiered pagoda tower. In the center of the square stood a couple of pagodas with statues of Hindu gods and goddesses inside, their roof beams carved with religious scenes. People prayed at the temples. At one of the pagodas, a priest rang a brass bell, its clear sound ringing through the cool mountain air.

“Impressive, isn’t it?” Agent Tamang said. “It’s one of the great royal squares of Nepal, although I think the one in Bhaktapur is better. That’s where my family is from. I grew up in Georgia but come back almost every year.”

He pointed to the long building of red stone with the tower. Jana studied it again, her expert eye catching countless details. Every inch of the woodwork was carved. “That was the royal palace of the Shah and Malla dynasties until the 19th century. And these temples are some of my favorites. Some date back five hundred years, although the historians say this square has been holy for more than a thousand years before that.” His voice turned soft. “These temples were terribly damaged in the last earthquake.”

“I saw the video,” Jana said. “Heartbreaking.”

“Temples can be repaired,” Detective Gurung said. “Nine thousand people got killed. Whole villages were flattened. At least the temples can be repaired.”

“Some look like they weren’t damaged at all,” Jacob said. “Did those guys fix them up?” He pointed to a team of artisans working on a temple encased in scaffolding. Several men were tapping away on wooden beams, making ornate carvings of Hindu deities, while others were pieced together what Jana could see were original pieces of the decoration.

"Them and many more," the detective said with obvious pride. "Nepalese artisans from all over the world came home to help. We all donated too."

Jana and Jacob fell silent. For all their globetrotting, for all the fights they'd had with secret societies and terrorist organizations, there were some disasters you couldn't predict and couldn't stop.

From the square, it was only a short walk to the antique shop along a bustling street lined with small shops. Some were obvious tourist traps, while others served the locals, selling clothing and household items. At number 5 hung a modest sign saying "Nepalese Mementoes and Antiques, Prakash Rai, proprietor."

From the outside, it looked like a regular tourist shop. Dusty windows displayed mass-produced bags embroidered with Tibetan designs, prayer wheels, statues of Shiva and Ganesh, and even some little brass vajras.

It looked like any one of a dozen tourist shops she'd seen in her brief stay in Nepal's capital city, but she had been dealing with the secret side of life long enough to know that appearances could be deceiving.

Jana and Jacob walked in alone. Agent Arjun Tamang and Detective Ram Gurung sat at an outdoor dumpling stand down the street, keeping an eye on everything. They had decided it would be better if just the two Americans went in, posing as tourists and feeling out the situation. The locals could always go in later and lean on him.

They entered through the glass door, Jana taking the lead. A little bell tinkled as they came inside. They found themselves in a narrow shop stretching back twenty feet to a counter. To one side was a display of incense and books on Buddhism, Hinduism, and Nepalese culture. On the other were racks of colorful clothing and handbags made for the tourist trade as well as the sacred-style objects like those displayed in the window. Jana wondered if a Buddhist monk or Hindu priest would consider them actual sacred objects. They looked the same, but the intent in their manufacture couldn't have been more different.

A thin Nepalese man with wild hair and even wilder eyes came out of the back room behind the counter.

"Hello. Welcome to my shop," he said in heavily accented English. "How may I help you?"

"Oh, we're just browsing," Jana said. It was hard to look into his eyes; they had such an intense gaze. "I'm interested in the history and archaeology of the Himalayan region."

"You might like some of my books, then." He gestured toward the bookshelf.

Jana perused the volumes. "These are nice, but they're a bit basic. I'm looking for something more detailed. Do you have any publications by the university?"

"Oh, we don't get much demand for those. I can give you the names of one or two bookshops that have a better selection. Are you ... interested in antiques?"

Jana glanced around. "You have antiques?"

There certainly weren't any in evidence, despite what the sign said.

Prakash Rai caught her glance and smiled. "Not these things, of course. I have a few objects here in the counter."

He pointed down at the glass-topped counter. Jana and Jacob walked over. Inside, they saw a variety of statuettes and small items of jewelry, some ornamented with semiprecious stones.

Jana was no expert on Asian antiquities, but she saw none of the obvious techniques for making new things look old. Sometimes shop owners would abrade an item to make it look worn, but the wear would never be in a natural pattern. At other times, they'd use a mildly acidic solution to stain it. This, too, was easily spotted because it didn't make the same color pattern as natural aging.

Still, these could be more clever forgeries. She couldn't see them well enough to tell for sure.

"That's a lovely Gawu box," she said, pointing to a little brass amulet inlaid with lapis lazuli.

"Oh, you are familiar with these?"

"Oh, yes. It holds an image of the Buddha," she said with more confidence than she felt. That crash course she had given herself on the flight over couldn't replace a proper knowledge of the region.

"Indeed, it does." He reached into the counter through an opening in the back and pulled it out.

Opening the front of the box, they saw a little jade Buddha set into the interior.

"This dates to the eighteenth century and was made in the west of my country."

Jana had no idea if that was true, but it was certainly impressive craftsmanship.

"Beautiful. I might get that, but I'd like to see what else you have. Do you have any masks or daggers?" She nudged Jacob. "My husband loves knives."

Jana's heart did a sudden flip-flop. Did she just refer to him as her husband?

Well, we are undercover, after all.

"Oh yes, I have some antique swords in the back. Come this way."

He opened up a little hatch in the counter so they could pass through. Beyond the doorway was a dimly lit room that was entirely different than the front.

Jana gasped with unfeigned delight. The room looked more like a museum.

Strange wooden masks hung on the walls, their faded paint not reducing the power of their artistry. A large prayer wheel that must have once hung in a temple or monastery rested upright on a shelf. Several swords, spears, and daggers hung on another wall. A couple of shelves held smaller items such as the jewelry and statuettes like those beneath the countertop.

"Impressive," Jana said. "Why don't you have these on display out front?"

Prakash Rai made a dismissive gesture toward the front room. "Those are for the regular tourists. Only visitors with true interest get to come back here."

Jana suspected he was buttering her up in anticipation of a sale. She hadn't shown much knowledge to get to see the back room, although she supposed the average young backpacker wouldn't have the interest or money to purchase these things.

She browsed a bit. Jacob played his part and examined the knives, staying close to an especially deadly-looking one. Jana picked up an ornate brass vajra from the shelf.

She let out a sigh. "A pity we didn't get to see the royal one. We just got here yesterday."

"Yes, it's a terrible shame," the proprietor said. Jana glanced at him and didn't see any evasion in his eyes.

The front door bell rang.

"Excuse me, I have another customer."

Prakash Rai moved out to the front room. Jana peeked through the doorway and saw a young Nepalese man with long hair standing in the doorway, hand on the doorknob. He looked hesitant. When Prakash said something in Nepali he replied, then looked at Jana.

Just then, something in the street caught his attention. He looked to his right, his eyes widened, and he bolted away to his left down the street, leaving the door hanging open.

A moment later, Agent Tamang and Detective Gurung sprinted down the street after him.

CHAPTER SIX

Jacob had no idea why he was chasing this guy, but if the local CIA agent and a local detective were both after him, that was good enough.

It had taken only a matter of moments to rush past Jana and that weirdo antiques dealer, vault over the counter, and get out the door.

Even so, his new Nepalese buddies and the suspect were way ahead of him.

The guy was sprinting down a busy street, though, and having to weave between local shoppers and photo-snapping tourists was slowing him down. That slowed Tamang and Gurung down too, but by the time the three guys had shouldered their way through the crowd, the crowd had parted enough to give Jacob a clear space to run.

He began to gain on them, or at least on the two local friendlies.

The suspect waited for a space in the traffic and angled across the street.

It was then that Jacob figured out why they were chasing him.

He was missing the tip of the ring finger on his left hand.

On the flight over, they had studied and restudied the security footage from the museum. Because the building was so new, it had top-shelf cameras that gave crystal clear images, not like the grainy, fuzzy images that had frustrated his investigation so many times before. While the men had all been masked, he and Jana had memorized certain features. The older man with a bit of a pot belly. The guy with a burn mark on his right hand. The unusually skinny guy.

And the guy with long hair is missing the tip of his left ring finger.

There couldn't be that many people in Kathmandu matching that description, and here he was showing up at the shop of an antique dealer who approached the man who probably knew about this enigmatic symbol the thieves had left at the crime scene.

Coincidence? Jacob didn't believe in coincidences. Certainly not one this big.

The terrorist cut down a side street. Jacob had caught up to Tamang and Gurung, and they chased him down there together.

They found themselves in a narrow alley between two wooden buildings. An open door let out a cloud of fragrant steam. Probably a kitchen. The suspect avoided it. Smart move. Too much of a chance of a dead end and he had a clear shot along the alley to the next street over. He had made the right decision.

Jacob laughed when it suddenly turned into the wrong one. A tuk tuk, one of the ubiquitous three-wheeled vehicles used as miniature taxis all over Asia, pulled up at the other end of the alley and stopped. The driver, oblivious to the drama happening in the alley, lit a cigarette.

The terrorist didn't skip a beat. He tucked his head and leapt right through the empty back seat and onto the street.

Detective Gurung shouted something in Nepali, flashing a badge. The driver stared, his cigarette falling from his gaping mouth, then hit the gas and got out of the way.

Too late, though. Those extra couple of seconds had let the suspect get far ahead.

He had run into a wide street filled with an open-air bazaar. Stalls lined either side, shaded by awnings. Crowds of shoppers picked through fruits, vegetables, heaps of cheap imported clothing from China, and household items.

Damn. He could shake us here easy.

Jacob had another problem too. He was already getting winded. While he had done a lot of operations in mountainous areas, he'd been at sea level for months and hadn't had time to get accustomed to Kathmandu's 1,400-meter elevation. Tamang and Gurung were beginning to pull ahead.

And the suspect had just disappeared into the crowd.

Jacob plunged into the same crowd behind his two Nepalese colleagues. The detective was shouting something, probably ordering everyone to get out of the way. They did, but too damn slowly. Jacob peered through the thicket of shoppers trying to spot their man.

There he was! He was crouching low, zigzagging through the crowd in the hope he wouldn't be spotted. This guy was a pro.

A damn good runner, too. And acclimatized. Nepalese tended to have big barrel chests holding oversized lungs. The thin air didn't bother them in the least.

Jacob was going to lose this race.

And then, some luck.

Mr. Missing Finger zigged when he should have zagged and rammed right into a woman carrying two heavy shopping bags. Down they both went.

The suspect was up in a flash, but then a man emerged from the crowd, swinging a fist.

An irate husband or brother? If so, he didn't help his relative's honor. Mr. Missing Finger gave him a right cross that laid him flat.

Another man moved in, and the guy nailed him with an elbow strike that knocked him out.

Detective Gurung must have decided that enough was enough. He drew his revolver and shouted something that sounded like a command to halt.

The suspect didn't halt. Instead, he ducked into the thickest part of the crowd.

Gurung said something that was most definitely a curse and chased after him, Agent Tamang right behind.

Jacob was lagging badly now, lungs heaving, but he had an idea. When the guy disappeared into a thick knot of people, he had dodged straight to the left. While that got him out of sight for the moment, it also hinted that his goal might be a narrow alley to one side of the street, just visible between a stall piled high with melons and another piled high with potatoes. Jacob guessed he was heading that direction.

Jacob angled for that same alley to cut him off.

He hoped he guessed right, because if the guy went any other direction there was no way Jacob would ever catch up.

Elbowing his way through the crowd, which was too thick to get out of the way in time, Jacob caught a glimpse of the suspect ducking between the two stalls, heading for the alley.

Jacob willed his weakening muscles and burning lungs to an extra effort and got to the alley entrance a moment after him. He grabbed the back of his shirt, and both men stumbled.

The terrorist spun around and clocked Jacob in the face with enough force to slam him into the corner of the building. Jacob soaked up another hit before he got his guard up, blocked two more attacks, and threw a weak punch of his own that didn't even come close to landing.

Jeez. I hope the next time I have a high-altitude mission that I get the chance to adjust first.

Assuming there is a next time.

Another blow got through Jacob's guard but this time Jacob managed a weak jab that smacked the guy on the chin. His opponent replied with a swing that Jacob barely managed to dodge, then a kick that Jacob had to leap back to avoid.

It turned out that was the plan. The guy turned and bolted down the alley. He must have seen how ragged Jacob looked and, knowing newcomers couldn't deal with the altitude, felt running was the better option.

Except the alley was far more crowded than the last one. Heaps of sacks and boxes, probably from the market stalls and the shops on either side of the alley, nearly blocked his way.

He leapt over some sacks, weaved between some rolled-up carpets, and scrambled up a stack of boxes as Jacob panted behind him. By the time Jacob got to the top of the stack of boxes, the guy was pelting down a clear spot in the alley a good ten feet ahead.

Time to change tactics.

Jacob lifted up one of the boxes, found it to be full of things that rattled and were fairly light, and tossed it at him.

Direct hit! The guy went down, the box shattered, and dozens of Buddhist prayer wheels scattered all over the alleyway.

Oops. Bad karma.

Jacob scrambled down the far side of the stack of boxes and ran up to him.

Just as the guy started getting up, Jacob knocked him down again. A few more swift punches kept him down. Jacob frisked him and found no weapons.

Fast footsteps behind him. Agent Tamang and Detective Gurung had figured out where the suspect had bolted to and joined the party. Neither looked winded at all.

"I … got … him … " Jacob panted, leaning against the alley wall. He hoped he wouldn't throw up. Not a good look.

"You need to adjust to our altitude," Agent Tamang said.

"How … long … does it … take you when … you fly … in from Georgia?"

The Nepali-American shrugged.

Detective Gurung pulled a pair of handcuffs from his pocket and bent to cuff the suspect. Just as he got in reach, the guy lashed out, kicking him in both kneecaps. Gurung cried out and fell. Within a flash, he had pulled the detective's gun from its holster.

A shot rang out, echoing loudly in the alleyway.

CHAPTER SEVEN

Jana had no idea why Agent Tamang, Detective Gurung, and then Jacob had run off chasing one of Prakash Rai's customers, but she could guess. The Nepalis thought he had been suspicious for whatever reason, and when they approached, he confirmed that by running off.

Innocent people don't run.

The antiques dealer stared at the door for a moment, then solemnly moved over to it and shut it.

Jana sucked in a breath and was about to bolt to the back room and grab the nearest knife. She hesitated, though, because he did not lock it, and the look he gave her was one of concern.

"Who are you?" he asked.

Jana made a quick calculation and decided that telling part of the truth might be the best approach.

"We're investigating the disappearance of Professor Suresh Joshi."

"And the theft of the Royal Vajra."

Jana tensed up again.

"Why do you think that?"

"Because I know why they stole it."

"Really? Why?"

"Who was that man at the door? The one your husband chased?"

"I don't know."

Prakash studied her for a moment. Jana couldn't tell if he believed her or not.

She decided to give him more. "Those two Nepalese men who ran past were policemen we're working with."

"So my government called in foreign help?"

"I'm an archaeologist. My … husband … is also an investigator."

"Do you have any identification?"

Jana pulled out one of the many fake IDs Jacob kept around the house like playing cards. This one said she was a member of Interpol.

He studied it a moment, looked at her, and then said,

"This is because I went to see Professor Joshi's wife, isn't it?"

Jana hesitated. How much to reveal?

She decided to show her hand. It seemed like the antiques dealer had already figured her out.

"The terrorists who stole the Royal Vajra spray-painted a symbol on the wall of the gallery. A specialist we spoke to said it was a *car mey*, an ancient symbol from the prehistoric rock art that Professor Joshi had been studying."

Prakash Rai didn't look surprised by this revelation, only excited.

"I knew it! I knew the *car mey* was the precursor to the vajra. I bet Professor Joshi knew it too, in the end."

"In the end?"

Prakash's face turned grim. He looked out the window of his shop either way down the street. Jana looked too. There was no sign of Jacob or the others, and no one seemed to be watching the storefront.

"Do you mind if I lock the door?" he asked.

"Go ahead."

Jana figured that if he was asking, then he wasn't a threat. She had become much better at judging people since her life had been regularly on the line for the past year.

He locked the door and then turned to her.

"Let's go to the back room. If that man your husband is chasing is really one of the thieves, there might be more around."

They went to the back room and sat on a pair of rickety old stools, surrounded by items from the region's past.

Prakash began to speak.

"The vajra, or the dorje as it's called in Tibetan, is an ancient symbol that stretches back to before Buddhism spread here from India in the seventh century. It … how much do you know of the history of this region?"

"Not much," Jana admitted. "I really was an archaeologist before joining Interpol, but I specialized in Roman archaeology."

Jana felt a peculiar sensation when she said her profession in the past tense. She wasn't sure if she was telling a lie or the truth.

"I see. Well, before Hinduism and Buddhism made it to Nepal, we had various pagan beliefs. The Tibetan plateau, being more isolated, maintained these earlier traditions until later, when Buddhist monks penetrated the area and brought the teachings of Buddha to the people. Only then did they get enlightened."

"You're a Buddhist?"

"Yes, although I find much wisdom in Hinduism as well. We don't have the religious intolerance here that you do in the West or the

Middle East. Even Tibetan Buddhism incorporates many ideas from the old religion, and it is wise to do so. The old ways contained hints at some the greatest of lost knowledge. But back to the vajra. It originates from the *cyar mey*, which symbolized pure power and energy. Only when it was incorporated into Buddhist philosophy did it take on spiritual aspects."

"So the pagan Tibetans saw it as a sort of lightning symbol?"

"That's what Dr. Joshi thought, at least at first. He and I came to know each other because he liked to collect Tibetan and Nepali antiques. Since he traveled so much for work and went to many remote places, he was in a better position than I am to find rare artifacts. Some he kept, while others he sold to me to sell to collectors. We had a business arrangement that soon turned into an intellectual collaboration."

"How so?"

"He talked to me about his survey of the remote caves in the Himalayas, and I talked to him about how they might contain traces of the advanced ancient civilization that existed around the world more than a hundred thousand years ago."

Jana shifted in her seat. This was the same nonsense the Antiquities Division had been talking about. They claimed that a civilization with advanced technology had thrived a hundred thousand years ago and wiped itself out. Most evidence of it got destroyed by the glaciers moving across the northern part of the globe in the last Ice Age, but traces could be found in the more remote regions of the planet.

There was no evidence that such a civilization had ever existed.

And yet, this strange man in a little shop in Kathmandu was telling the same story.

Maybe it was just some popular conspiracy theory. Jana didn't pay any attention to that sort of stuff.

"I can see you don't believe me," Prakash Rai said. "Professor Joshi didn't believe me either until he started finding the caves."

Jana remembered that cave Bledshaw had shown her in rural India. The cave contained strange paintings that seemed to show hovercraft and bacteria as seen through a microscope. The amount of lime that had hardened over the images in this limestone cave indicated a great age, but a number of variables could account for that and she had remained unconvinced.

The antiques dealer went on.

“At first, he only found primitive drawings, the kind of crude depictions of hunters and animals that you find in all early cave art. Nothing as good as what you have in Europe at caves such as Lascaux and Altamira, but interesting enough and worthy of study. It was only when he ventured further into the isolated valleys and high up on the peaks that he found something truly important.

“There he found caves showing things he never thought he’d find—airplanes and submarines, sketches of electric circuits. He thought he had gone mad from altitude sickness, or he had been fooled by some pranksters, but the photos he took and the isolation of the widely separated caves convinced him that what he was seeing was real. The descendants of that great fallen civilization were drawing what they could no longer create as a sort of memorial to an age gone by.

“He became secretive of his findings, fearing that his colleagues would think of him as a crank. The administration at the university is very strict and wouldn’t condone such an embarrassment. He might have lost his job. But there was one person he knew he could talk to. Me. I have been studying esoteric texts all my life and have found convincing evidence of an early civilization that was as advanced, and in many ways more advanced, than we are.”

Jana cut in. "A civilization that wiped itself out, and then most of the evidence for it disappeared under the glaciers of the last Ice Age."

Prakash raised an eyebrow. “You’ve know of this.”

“I’ve heard people talking about it.”

“And you remain unconvinced.”

Jana looked him in the eye. “Yes.”

The antiques dealer sighed. “If only you had seen those photos. He and his graduate student tried to explain them away, but they were both intelligent men and eventually had to believe the evidence before them, especially when they found such drawings in five different caves. The Sherpas who led them to the caves already believed. The more remote tribes up there have never lost the memory of true history.”

“And what is that?”

Prakash grimaced. “Still that doubt, and yet you came all the way here. I think a part of you wants to believe.”

“What is this true history and how does it link with the theft of the Royal Vajra and that weird *cyar mey* symbol on the museum wall?”

She was beginning to lose patience. People who claimed to have rare information often acted superior. She sure saw it a lot in academia, and she had been seeing it lately among people who studied esoterica.

Prakash ignored her tone and went on.

"The *car mey* was the predecessor to the vajra, as I said, and it symbolized raw power. It wasn't exactly electric power, although the ancients used the lightning bolt as part of its symbol. They did this because they had no other visual marker to refer it to. But the power was something beyond electricity, a greater power coming from the earth itself."

"You're talking about ley lines?"

Try as she might, Jana couldn't hide the contempt in her voice.

"Ley lines are not the power, they are the grid, and the modern concept of ley lines is only part of the truth. There is great energy within the earth, and the ancients were able to tap into it and power their entire civilization. It was dangerous work, though, and so they put their power in the most remote areas possible. One spot was high in the Himalayas. I think Professor Joshi was close to that spot, and that's why they took him."

"You mean the same people who took the Royal Vajra?"

He nodded solemnly. "The Royal Vajra is far older than the academics believe. It is an artifact from that ancient civilization. It is part of the mechanism that taps into the energy and then can be channeled to good uses … or bad ones."

"And you're thinking Dr. Joshi figured this out and so the terrorists kidnapped him, maybe to force him to help figure out how to use this ancient energy?"

Jana couldn't believe her own ears. Was she seriously entertaining this crazy idea?

Ridiculous. On the other hand, people believed in all kinds of ridiculous things. If the thieves believed it, she would have to think along these same lines in order to catch them.

"I think so," Prakash said.

"There are two things you haven't thought of. The first is that Professor Joshi didn't even believe in this ancient civilization until quite recently. How much could he help?"

"I don't know. Maybe they have other artifacts they want him to interpret. Or maybe they want him to lead them to the caves."

"The second problem is that they spray painted the *car key* in the same place they stole the Royal Vajra. Why tip us off?"

Prakash Rai rubbed his jaw for a moment, looking down at the floor.

At last, he responded, "I don't know. You're correct that it makes no sense, but they must have had a reason."

CHAPTER EIGHT

Agent Tamang stood over the suspect, his gun in his hand. The suspect lay sprawled on his back with a surprised expression on his face and a neat hole in his forehead.

Detective Gurung said something in Nepali that sounded like a thank you and retrieved his gun.

Jacob couldn't believe it. He had screwed up big time. He should have made sure the guy was truly unconscious, and he should have held him in an armlock until Detective Gurung had him cuffed.

Instead, he had simply stood there panting like a tourist on his first day of a Himalayan hike, thinking the fight was over.

He knew better than that. The fight was never over.

And when the suspect knocked Gurung down and grabbed his gun in his hand, Jacob could have kicked it out of his hand, or kicked him in the side of the head, but he had hesitated for a crucial half second.

If Agent Tamang hadn't been so quick on the draw, they'd all be dead.

He had frozen, just like in the last mission.

What's happening to me?

"I'm sorry," he gasped with lungs still heaving. "I am so sorry."

"It's all right," Tamang said.

"I'm sorry."

"It could have happened to anyone. He was so quick," Gurung added.

"God I screwed up."

"No, you didn't." they both said.

Yeah, he had.

Maybe he had burnt out. The job got to some agents. Something would happen, sometimes something they didn't notice at the time, that threw them off. They lost their edge and became a liability.

Have I really become a liability?

"I'm sorry," he said again. He didn't know what else to say.

"There was no way you could have known," Gurung said, "and no way you could have disarmed him in time."

Maybe they meant it. A lot of field operatives wouldn't have been able to do that.

But he was Jacob Snow. He could have done it. *Should* have done it.

***

Half an hour later, he had regained his breath but not his confidence. The police had come to deal with the body, and they had gone back to the antiques shop.

At least Jana was on the ball. She'd gotten the weird antiques dealer to talk, and damn did he have a lot to say. Now they all sat in a cramped back room of his shop, drinking tea he had brewed for them as he related everything he'd told Jana.

Poor Jana. Back to this ancient advanced super-civilization. She had a hard time swallowing that. He did too, but that Indian cave and the stuff in the hydroelectric dams had made him half believe it. Easier for him. He didn't have years of academic training to limit his thinking.

Or make it sharper. Perhaps this was all bullshit, and only she had the knowledge to see through it.

Glancing at Tamang and Gurung, he saw a pair of poker faces. He was wearing one too. He'd have to talk to them later. See what the locals thought of all this. The local perspective was always vital, especially when he was in a region unfamiliar to him.

Which made him wonder, why send him at all? Tyler Wallace had said the Chinese were keeping an eye on all the local agents, but Tamang had been called up to help. It seemed like Wallace wanted him and Jana specifically for this mission.

Did he have some inkling that it might involve the Antiquities Division and the Professor Harlow?

It was sure shaping up that way.

Prakash Rai had opened up a cabinet and brought out a heap of old books, flipping through various pages to show pictures and read passages of text.

The *car mey* appeared in a few of them. Once carved into a rock on a high pass near Mount Everest. Another painted on the wall of the oldest monastery in Tibet, later destroyed in the Chinese invasion of 1950. A third image was only a crude drawing made by a Buddhist monk five hundred years ago, which he said he had seen in an ancient manuscript.

Prakash read the account from this last volume.

"This book was published in 1926, but the account is from the fifteenth century. The monk says, 'In a distant monastery in the Ngari region'—that's in western Tibet—'I happened upon an old chest covered in dust and cobwebs hidden beneath the stairs. The abbot claimed he had never seen this chest and granted permission for me to open it, for he was just as curious as I as to its contents. Inside, we found many manuscripts of faded paper bound with string and covered in wood. We found an old copy of the Book of the Dead, as well as a history of the monastery that contained information about its early years not known to even the eldest and most learned among the monks. But by far the most enlightening was a manuscript of great age, said to be a copy of one centuries older, that recounted tales of the Ancient Kingdom of Great Wisdom and Folly.'"

"What's that?" Jacob asked, sipping the tea he'd been given.

"I've heard this name before," the antiques dealer said. "The Ancient Kingdom of Great Wisdom and Folly comes up a few times in the oldest manuscripts in the Himalayas and refers to the prehistoric civilization we've been talking about. Scholars think it's a mythical place, a metaphor for a higher time when people were purer and more enlightened. A select few know it was as real as the Roman empire."

Jacob glanced at his lover. She did not look convinced or happy.

Prakash Rai continued to read the monk's account.

"The manuscript contained many tales of that great and noble kingdom, ones that we should all study to gain insight into man's ability to be wise and foolish at the same time. One which I found especially insightful tells of how the kingdom came to its final end. The scholars of the kingdom used the *cyar mey* to power their flying chariots and the manmade suns that lit their cities and turned night into day. Although the great cities of The Ancient Kingdom of Great Wisdom and Folly were far to the north in the lands where snow fell in the valleys in winter, they kept the *cyar mey* in our land, in the remotest mountains, because they feared its power and wished to keep it away from their people like a blacksmith keeps the sparks from his forge away from his silo of barley."

Jacob glanced at Jana. She was frowning, but at least she was listening.

Prakash went on reading the old monk's writings.

"The power created by the *cyar mey* was able to pass through the ground in different directions like the water from underground springs, to rise up in those distant northern lands and be used for all manner of purposes. The Ancient Kingdom of Great Wisdom and Folly grew wealthy and powerful because of this power, and ruled over the world even though they did not extend their settlements much beyond the north.

"But wealth is the great deceiver, and makes men fight among themselves. Despite the plenty in their cities, some wanted more. Some wanted to rule in the place of those who were in power, and they hatched a plan to do so. Among them were some of the scholars who manipulated and channeled the *cyar mey*, and they decided to snuff out the great power like one snuffs out a candle, to make the rulers of the kingdom defenseless while the warriors among the rebels assaulted the palace. After they had seized power, they planned to rekindle the power and rule over all.

"It was folly, as all of men's plans based on desire turn out to be. The rulers had feared such a thing might come to pass, and so they had guards hidden at the source of the *cyar mey*. When the rebels tried to snuff it out, they were attacked. A great fight ensued, with both sides wielding the power of the *cyar mey*. In the end, both lost, felled by the power they struggle to control, and the *cyar mey* itself blew out like a candle when someone opens a door on a windy day.

"The Ancient Kingdom of Great Wisdom and Folly fell. Deprived of its power, the flying chariots plummeted from the air, the metal fish they rode in sank into the sea. Their cities went dark. The savage people who had hunted and gathered beyond their walls, looking in hungrily, burst inside and slaughtered them all. Thus ended the kingdom, like all edifices of man built on pride. Remember, oh brothers seeking the path to Enlightenment, remember this tale and keep close to the path set out by the Buddha. Reject earthly things, for men much cleverer than you and I have been brought down by them."

Prakash Rai closed the book with a solemn air. "The gunmen who took the Royal Vajra want to restart the *cyar mey*. If they can, they'd have more power than the Chinese and Indian armies combined."

Everyone sat for a moment in silence. Jacob turned to Agent Tamang and Detective Gurung.

"Can I talk to you guys alone for a moment?"

They nodded and went to the front room, leaving Jana with the antiques dealer.

"What do you think?" Jacob asked in a low voice.

Agent Tamang let out a long, slow breath, raising his eyebrows.

"I think we got a nutcase on our hands," the Nepalese-American said.

"Don't be so quick to dismiss it," Detective Gurung snapped. "It's a metaphor, sure, but spiritual power is real."

"What's definitely real is that symbol spray painted on the museum wall," Jacob said. "Let's set aside whether it's true or not for the moment and look into how this might give us a lead."

The two Nepalese nodded. Agent Tamang looked as unconvinced as Jana, but saw the logic in what Jacob was saying.

Jacob wished he could brief his two companions on what he'd learned on the last mission, but that was highly classified.

It all fit, and he had a feeling that Professor Harlow was behind this.

He had proved a ruthless enemy in the past, killing tens of thousands of people to get his way.

Jacob knew he'd do it again, or worse.

CHAPTER NINE

A remote mountain pass on the Nepal/Chinese border
That same day

Huddled in his clifftop observation post, Private Nagesh Agrawal peered through the mist, trying to see the border. He could just make out the bottom of the slope he was on, the nearest bunker, and the rough valley floor beyond. He couldn't even see the path leading to the border.

A path, not a road. This pass was too remote, too high in altitude, for anyone to have ever built a road here.

Still, it was a pass, and the Chinese could conceivably march an army through here if they really wanted to be cruel to their men and lose half of them to frostbite and exhaustion.

Private Agrawal was cold, bored, and homesick. For the thousandth time, he told himself he was stupid for joining the Nepalese army.

Agrawal came from a remote village where people farmed and didn't do much else. He always craved something more and dreamed of life in a big city like Kathmandu or even New Delhi.

A cousin's experiences had cured him of that. Gajendra had gone and worked as a cook in Kathmandu, did well, and then moved south to work in a restaurant in New Delhi. His Indian boss had fooled him into investing his pay in what was supposed to be a bank but was really a scam. Then the boss fired Gajendra on a made-up excuse. Gajendra was left broke. When he went to the police, he was beaten and told to "go home, you dirty Nepalese."

Nagesh Agrawal decided to join the army instead. You got a gun, a snappy uniform, better pay than anyone in the village, and the chance to travel. Some even got into the UN forces and went all the way to the Middle East and Africa, coming back with chests covered in medals.

None of that happened. Instead, he'd spent the last two years in this horrible place. His parents would write him letters, precious letters he'd read over and over again, telling him news of the village and how everyone was so proud of him for defending the nation's borders.

Defending what? A miserable, windswept mountain pass of virtually no strategic value?

Beyond the clammy mantle of mist—a daily occurrence here—he knew the valley floor angled up slightly to a low ridge, then back down again. The border was at the ridge, guarded by a pair of concrete blockhouses, one on the Nepalese side and the other on the Chinese side. On the edges of the valley to either side were bunkers and "lookout posts" like the miserable shelter he shivered in. But with this mist, half the time, the lookouts couldn't see a thing.

He wished he was home. The village didn't seem so bad anymore.

The crack of a rifle shot woke him out of his self-pity. It sounded like it came from the Chinese side of the border. The shot echoed down the valley like a ghostly volley.

Private Agrawal gripped his rifle, tense, poised.

His radio crackled to life, and his captain's voice came over the air. "Who was that? Who's firing?"

Before anyone could answer, several more shots rang out, then the thud of an RPG round.

A full-scale attack!

What should he do? His orders were to stay at his post, and yet he couldn't see anything. His friends, his comrades were down there and stuck where he was, he couldn't do a thing to help.

The rattle of a machine gun decided him. He had to get down there.

Ducking out the back of his shelter, he began to pick his way down the narrow path leading to the valley floor. Private Agrawal decided he'd go to the nearest bunker and reinforce them.

He hadn't made it halfway there before a fusillade of gunshots and a trio of RPG rounds reverberated from his right.

From his right? That was behind their lines! Had the Chinese flanked them?

But how? There wasn't another path for at least twenty-five miles, and the captain was in constant radio communication with all the border posts.

An explosion trembled the mountain, and the mist flared a garish red.

That came from the direction of the command post!

Risking a fall that could break his neck, Agrawal sprinted the rest of the way down to the bunker. He got to the steel door at the back and pounded on it.

"Let me in!"

The door opened, and Corporal Rajan stared at him.

"I can't see a thing up there," Agrawal explained. "I came to help you."

The corporal pulled him in and slammed the door shut.

Inside were two privates, a heavy machine gun, and a radio that was a chaotic jabber of a dozen screaming voices.

"What's going on?" Agrawal asked, getting to one of the firing slits and flicking off the safety to his AK-47.

"No idea," the corporal said. "They flanked us somehow. We have to—"

Another explosion rocked the mountain pass.

Agrawal peered through the firing slit. From here he could see much of the valley, but not far enough through the mist to see the border line. Smoke came up from a bunker close to the border, but oddly he saw no movement. Shouldn't the Chinese be charging over the ridge?

He glanced the other direction, down the Nepalese side of the valley, and saw an orderly line of figures charging up out of the mist. They kept in formation, widely spaced so as to make a poor target.

"There!"

Agrawal snapped off a shot, the sound deafening in the confines of the small concrete bunker.

"Hold your fire!" Corporal Rajan ordered. "They're still out of range."

The two privates manning the machine gun swung their weapon in the direction of the advancing line and got ready.

Another explosion, and dimly through the mist they could see smoke rising from the bunker on the opposite side of the valley.

Private Agrawal glanced back at the Chinese side of the border. No movement there. No firing. What was going on?

Then he focused on the line of figures advancing up the valley toward them. They didn't wear Chinese uniforms, or indeed Nepalese ones.

They didn't wear uniforms at all.

"All right," Corporal Rajan said with a grim voice, "they're almost within range. Nagesh, you and I will take out the guys on the right of the line. Machine gunners, aim for the center. Just a few more seconds now."

Private Agrawal aimed down the barrel of his gun, picking out a target. The man didn't carry a rifle but something bulkier. Not an RPG but something bigger. Better take him out first. Agrawal didn't feel fear anymore, only a strange sense of detachment. This was it. He never thought he'd see combat but it had come. He would do his duty and defend his nation against … whoever these people were.

The line of attackers stopped. The one Agrawal was aiming at dropped to one knee and rested the bulky object on his shoulder.

"He's going to fire!" Corporal Rajan shouted.

That was the only order they needed. Everyone opened up.

The man didn't fall. They were still at long range and all their bullets missed.

A tongue of flame flicked out of the thing on the enemy's shoulder. There was a loud whoosh, an impact, and Private Nagesh Agrawal knew no more.

CHAPTER TEN

A remote valley in north-central Nepal
That same day

Ten-year-old Pemba Yanjee herded her sheep along the steep slope, her strong legs helping her hop from rock to rock and stroll across the thirty-degree angle with ease. The sheep liked it up here because there were clusters of bushes with sweet berries to eat. Yanjee liked it here because she could get a clear view of the whole valley and all the interesting things happening in it.

Far over at one end of the valley stood her village where her family and all her neighbors lived. In front of it, she could make out the barley fields and the little river that gave them water. Along one side of the valley ran the dirt road. She had seen pictures of paved roads, but she had never gone far enough outside this valley to see one with her own eyes.

If Yanjee looked the other way, she could see the snow-capped peaks shining in the sunlight.

All of these things were familiar and beautiful, but the most interesting thing of all was just down the slope from her.

The foreigners and their excavation.

Until they showed up, Yanjee had never heard of an excavation. An excavation is when people interested in the past dig into old ruins to find out what had happened before. Carol had explained it to her. Carol was her foreigner friend. She ran the excavation and spoke Sherpa.

When Yanjee had first come to stare at the excavation with the other village children, Carol had come right up to her and said hello in their own language. That amazed them all, and they were even more amazed when Carol kept speaking. She said some things in a funny way, and sometimes got her words mixed up, but she spoke pretty well.

Yanjee decided she'd help Carol learn to speak the language of the Sherpa better and Carol could teach her some English.

So every evening after Yanjee brought the sheep back and made sure the stall was securc, she'd hurry down to the excavation and speak with Carol. All the foreigners would smile at her, and the Nepalese workers would say hello. The workers had a happy little puppy Yanjee liked to play with. Then Yanjee and Carol would sit by the fire, eating Carol's chocolate and teaching each other their languages.

Yanjee had learned "hello" and "good evening" and "puppy" and "excavation" and many other words. Including "chocolate." That was her favorite word.

Carol would also show her around the excavation, explaining how the squares and trenches they had made in the rocky, shallow soil revealed the foundations of an old monastery that had stood here five hundred years ago. Yanjee remembered her grandfather telling her tales of the great monastery from long ago, but even he wasn't old enough to have ever seen it.

Carol also showed her the little plastic bags that held what she called "artifacts". Artifacts was a really hard word to say right and it meant old things found in an excavation. Some of the artifacts were boring like the pieces of pottery, but others were really pretty like the little porcelain Buddha and the pieces of carved wood. Yanjee asked for some, but Carol said they belonged to everybody and would be shown in a museum one day. "Museum" was another word Yanjee learned.

She could see them hard at work now, dust rising from the squares and trenches they were digging to uncover more of the old monastery. Yanjee squinted and tried to pick out Carol, but the excavation was too far away. Then one dumb sheep tried to wander off and Yanjee had to chase it and thwap it with her stick to get it back to the rest of the flock.

When she next had a chance to look down at the excavation, she saw a plume of dust along the road. Someone was coming in a car or truck.

Yanjee watched, curious. Hardly any vehicles came up the road. She saw a Land Rover and a truck. Maybe more workers for the excavation?

The Land Rover and truck drove right up to the edge of the excavation and parked. The excavation workers got out of their trenches and squares and stood looking at them.

Suddenly Yanjee felt worried. Something seemed wrong. The workers didn't look like they had been expecting these vehicles. They didn't go over to greet them like usual.

Then Yanjee spotted Carol. She had just climbed out of a square and was walking toward the vehicles, wiping her hands on her pants.

The doors to the Land Rover opened, and several men got out. Something in their hands gleamed in the sun, but Yanjee couldn't see what they held. Excavation tools?

Then, men came pouring out of the back of the truck. Something glinted in their hands too.

Carol backed up, then fell. Other workers on the excavation started falling, too. She spotted the puppy as a tiny dot running away across the fields.

Yanjee stared. What was going on?

Then the sharp mountain air carried to her the crackle of gunfire.

Yanjee screamed and ran back to her village.

CHAPTER ELEVEN

Jana awoke early to the sound of her phone ringing. The local CIA agent had given both her and Jacob SIM cards for the Nepalese phone system. She rubbed her eyes and reached over for her phone.

On the other side of the bed, Jacob rolled over and grabbed his phone too. Only when she saw that did she realize that both their phones were going off.

As she answered, she glanced at the window. The first golden light of dawn was just peeking through the shutters. She hadn't gotten enough sleep and she suspected she wasn't going to for a while.

"Hello?"

"Hello, Ms. Peters. This is Detective Ram Gurung. I'm terribly sorry to call you so early after such a long flight, but there's been a development."

"A development?" she asked, rubbing her eyes and sitting up. Her mind was still fogged with sleep.

"There's been an attack on an archaeological excavation."

"What?"

"A Canadian field crew in the north-central part of the country at the foothills to the higher peaks was attacked by a gang of masked men bearing AK-47s. They slaughtered every member of the crew, both the Canadians and the Nepalese workers. They didn't take any hostages, but they did take most of the artifacts."

"What were they excavating?"

"A medieval monastery."

Jana felt a chill go through her.

"We need to go there. Right now."

"I've already arranged a helicopter. We will pick you up in fifteen minutes."

"We'll be ready. Thank you."

Jana hung up. A moment later, she heard Jacob say, "thanks" and hang up too.

"What's going on?" Jacob asked.

"A field crew excavating a monastery got wiped out and the gunmen stole the artifacts."

“Jesus.”

“Who called you?”

"Tamang. He says there was an attack on a Nepalese army border post. Everyone got killed. The Chinese are denying responsibility, but the Nepalese government is livid. They're due to make a public announcement any minute and bring it up in the UN."

“Do you want to go up there?”

"Yes. Tamang asked but it's no-go. They're sending an entire regiment of troops to guard the pass, and they don't want a pair of CIA agents with eyeballs on the scene, even ones they've invited into the country."

“Have the Chinese crossed the border?”

“Unclear.”

Jana’s heart leapt. “So there might be an invasion?”

“Unclear. There aren’t any reports of other attacks on the border.”

“Strange.”

“Yeah. Not sure what’s going on. Tamang will keep us in the loop. So do you want to go to the excavation?”

“Detective Gurung has already arranged for a helicopter. He’s picking us up in fifteen minutes.”

Jacob nodded. “I like these guys. They’re on their toes.”

"They're going to have to be. We're getting into a whirlwind of drama, and I don't think it's going to stop any time soon."

Neither said anything more as they got dressed.

***

Three hours later, Jana stood at the edge of an archaeological excavation in a remote valley inhabited by a lone Sherpa village, fifty miles from the nearest highway. She was trying very hard not to vomit.

Bodies littered the field site, lying sprawled on the ground all around. A cluster of them were huddled in the furthest trench from the road, obviously having hoped they could hide there from their attackers.

They had been found and slaughtered where they crouched.

Several soldiers and rural police stood guard. A crowd of local villagers stood at some distance away, staring at the terrible scene.

The local police sergeant spoke to Jana with Detective Gurung as translator. Jacob had come, but Agent Tamang had stayed in Kathmandu to monitor the situation with the Chinese border incident.

"A witness says a Land Rover and a truck came up to the excavation right about there on the road, and men piled out with guns and opened fire without provocation. Then they appeared to have gone into that dig house over there and took most of the artifacts. It's nearly empty."

The police sergeant led them over to a shed. They had to wend their way between the bodies, Canadians and Nepalese side by side on the ground where they had once worked together. Jana kept her eyes averted, although it felt like a betrayal somehow. With all her dealings with the CIA, what if someone had targeted one of her excavations? Maybe it was good she had taken a break from archaeology.

But these people hadn't been CIA. They had been regular researchers, like she used to be.

One glimpse inside the shed told her the sergeant was right. Crates lay in disarray everywhere, empty or with their contents strewn on the floor. The gunmen had left behind the potsherds and various smaller items but seem to have taken much more. She didn't know what because the notes seemed to be gone too. They'd have to do a thorough search of the site and the camp to make sure.

Jana left the shed and looked around the excavation. Something strange caught her eye.

She walked over. The wall stood three courses high, high enough that at least the uppermost blocks would have been above ground and visible from the interior of the monastery when it was still in use. Indeed, from the baulk wall of the trench she could see the tamped earth floor of the monastery as a thin, hard line between layers of softer soil.

Three of the stone blocks had been pulled out of the upper course of the stone wall. She could tell because the edges of the surrounding stones were clean and unweathered.

Jacob came up to her. "Find something?"

He was already looking at the fresh hole in the wall.

"The attackers took something more than just the artifacts."

Jacob nodded, looking confused. "Maybe some art or an inscription?"

In several spots there were religious paintings and writing on the inside of the wall. They had all been covered by tarps to protect them from the elements, but those tarps had been torn away.

"That's what I'm thinking," Jana replied.

A police officer came up and said something to the local sergeant. Detective Gurung translated.

"We have a witness to the shooting. The only one who was close enough to have seen clearly what happened."

"Let's go see him."

"Her. A little shepherd girl who was tending her flock on the hillside over there."

Jana winced. A child saw this massacre?

They walked over to the crowd of villagers. A Sherpa man stood in front, his hands on the shoulders of a trembling barefoot girl clutching a puppy.

"She looks terrified," Jana said. "Detective Gurung, let's you and me just go up. The rest of you hang back."

"All right," the detective said.

The two of them went over to the girl and her father. Jana leaned over and smiled at her. The girl's bottom lip trembled. It was obvious she had been crying. Her father said some soothing words and stroked her hair.

"I'm Jana. What's your name?"

"Pemba Yanjee." The answer came out as such a soft whisper Jana barely heard her.

"How old are you, Pemba?"

When Detective Gurung translated, she called her Yanjee instead of Pemba. Jana noted the cultural difference for later use.

"Ten."

"That's a nice puppy. Can I pet it?"

"All right."

Jana petted the puppy. "She's cute. What's her name?"

"Carol."

"What did you see, Yanjee?"

The girl burst into tears. "They killed my friends!"

It took some time for the father to calm the girl down. Jana stood there, helpless, her eyes filling. Once the father had soothed her for a while, Yanjee went on.

"I was tending my sheep and watching the excavation." Jana blinked when she said the last word in English. "Some men came up in a truck and a Land Rover and shot everybody!"

"Did you see anything else?"

"I ran. After a while I looked back and none of the archaeologists were moving anymore." Yanjee said the word 'archaeologists' in

English. "I saw the men going through their bags and pockets, and then they searched all around the excavation squares."

These last two words were also said in English.

That's when the penny dropped. Yanjee had obviously been visiting the field crew and learning English. She meant it when she said they were her friends.

"Did you see what they took?"

"They took something from everybody's pocket, and took some things in the bags too. Then one let out a cheer and pointed to that wall over there." She pointed to the wall where some blocks had been removed. "They were very excited. A bunch of the men rushed over there and broke something off. They searched all around the trench, and that's when I decided to run back to the village and call for help. I didn't see anything else."

"Did you see what it was they were so interested in?"

The girl shook her head and held the puppy closer to her.

"No. I was too far. There are a lot of pictures on the walls. Maybe they took one of those."

Smart girl.

"Do you remember what kind of picture was over there?" Jana pointed to the broken wall.

"No. They excavated that yesterday, just before … before … "

She buried her face in the puppy's fur.

"Thank you, Yanjee. You've been very brave."

Jana gave her shoulder a squeeze, nodded a thanks to her father, and walked away.

"The sergeant tells me the other villagers only saw the shooting from a distance," Detective Gurung said. "They confirm that it was a Land Rover and a truck coming up from the other end of the valley. Witnesses from other villages along this road confirm that the two vehicles came from the highway fifty miles away. They didn't stop anywhere along the route, and we got no clear descriptions of the passengers."

"I wonder what they were searching in their pockets and bags for?"

"The sergeant already discovered the answer to that. All of their phones are missing."

Jana took in a sharp breath. "And you've found no cameras either, have you?"

The detective nodded. "Whatever was on that wall, they didn't want anyone to know."

"But how could they have known it had been excavated that very same day? Oh! They had an insider."

"That makes sense. But all the crew are accounted for, so unless it was one of the villagers, which the testimony of the girl seems to refute, then the gunmen killed their informant."

"I've seen that before," Jana said with a sigh. "We need to do a thorough search of the site. Look under the bodies. Look in the tents. Hell, look in the latrine. When there's a major find on a dig, everyone gathers around and takes pictures. We need to find a phone. The gunmen didn't stay long. Maybe they missed one."

"Good idea. The sergeant was planning on doing so after we get photos of the crime scene. We'll hurry that process along and get to work."

Jana looked around the scene of the massacre and shuddered. She remembered all the digs she'd been on. The hard work interspersed with joking around. The easy camaraderie of a group of people thrown together to do a tough job in a remote location. The romances that bloomed, and all the petty rivalries. All those things made memories that people carried with them for the rest of their lives.

For all that to end so violently, so needlessly …

"I'll find out who did this," she whispered to the field of corpses. "I'll get you justice."

CHAPTER TWELVE

Back in Kathmandu that evening, Jacob had a meeting with Agent Arjun Tamang, the local CIA operative. They met at the U.S. embassy in a soundproofed room. Not that they feared the Nepalese government spying on them, but the Chinese had built their brand-new embassy suspiciously close.

"There's been a development," Tamang said. "One of my contacts is a smuggler and he has a contact within the Nepalese People's Liberation Front. The Communists make much of their money by smuggling drugs like a lot of insurgent groups do."

"Liberating the people by getting them hooked?"

"Something like that. Anyway, he knows a guy in the group who's been rattled by the theft of the Royal Vajra and the border attack. The announcement this morning hit the nation like a nuclear warhead. Everyone's hating the Communists right now. Some people think that it was them who attacked the border post, since the Chinese deny involvement and they actually haven't crossed the border."

"How likely is that?"

"It's impossible to tell without investigating the battlefield, and the government isn't allowing anyone in and they're not saying anything. In any case, this guy is all rattled and thinks the whole crew is going to be rooted out and so he's made a deal. He's been granted immunity and a U.S. visa in exchange for telling us the location of a Communist cell right here in Kathmandu."

"Us, as in the Americans?"

"Yup. Didn't trust his own government not to throw him in prison. The deal hinges on his information being correct, and I'd like to check it out."

"Without telling the Nepalese security forces."

"It would only muddy the waters, and the guy won't cooperate if we do. If we find out anything useful, we can tell them afterwards."

"They won't be too happy about us performing ops in their territory."

"They'll be happy we took out a terror cell and, hopefully, got them some useful intel. You got to understand the government here, Jacob.

They're ruling an impoverished and underpopulated nation stuck between two huge regional superpowers. While they want to appear to do everything themselves to maintain their dignity and votes, they'll take any help they can get. Their invitation for you to come here and go around armed is a tacit approval of any action that helps them. Within reason, of course."

"Speaking of weapons, we never had time to get any yesterday."

"I got you an MP5 and a 9mm automatic. I heard those are your favorite weapons. Plus we'll take some stun grenades along on this operation. We've got a closet full of helmets and Kevlar for you to try on. I can fit out Jana as well."

"She's still with the cops. They found a phone underneath a pile of bodies the gunmen had missed. Now they're coming back to Kathmandu to crack it."

"Do they need our help with that?"

"It's one of the worker's phones. It's not encrypted. Any cell phone store will be able to crack it. The police won't have any problem."

"Good. Our informant gave us a sketch of the terrorist safe house. It's on the edge of town in a residential area. Let's move in late at night when they're asleep. There's only supposed to be five of them, lightly armed, so if we get the drop on them, we should be able to subdue them easily enough."

"Sounds like a plan. You have combat experience?"

"I fought with the 10th Mountain Division in Afghanistan. You ever get over there?"

Jacob shifted in his seat and tried desperately to maintain a poker face. He had been a Ranger in that theater, and when his unit perpetrated a massacre in an Afghani village where they had been ambushed, Jacob had cracked and killed several of his own men. He had gone rogue, feral, killing Taliban and any U.S. troops sent to capture him.

He couldn't remember much of those days. At last, the U.S. had sent their best operative to take him out.

Aaron Peters, Jana's father.

Aaron stalked him for days and watched as Jacob took out a group of Taliban fighters. Then one day a shepherd boy had taken a potshot at him. Jacob didn't remember this, but apparently he had jumped the boy, disarmed him, and let him go.

That act of mercy told Aaron that there was still some humanity left in Jacob Snow, and so instead of killing him as per orders, he incapacitated him, brought him home and, after months of therapy, convinced his superiors in the CIA to give him a new identity and a new job.

And now he was Agent Jacob Snow with the CIA.

Tamang, a fellow veteran, was still waiting for an answer.

"Yeah … I was there."

Tamang gave him a sympathetic look that made Jacob squirm.

Arjun probably thinks I went through some trauma. He has no idea how much trauma I inflicted on others.

"It's in the past, buddy," the Nepalese-American said. "Let's get on with the current mission and do some good."

Do some good. Yeah. I still have a lot of bad to balance out.

***

The Communist safe house stood on an acre of open land at the outer edges of Kathmandu's residential district, a spot where there were still many empty lots and the traffic was sparse. Many of the buildings were working-class apartments where the residents had to walk a long way to the nearest bus stop. The lucky few with cars kept them in locked garages. Streetlights only lit the main roads, and most streets, including the one where the safe house was located, only got ambient light from the other buildings.

The Communists had chosen property well. Jacob doubted they saw many police patrols in this area.

It was nearing midnight, and the streets had been quiet for a while now.

Except for the dog chained to the safe house front lawn. It barked at anything getting close, whether it was a stray cat or their car when they had driven slowly by.

"Don't worry," Arjun Tamang said as he parked two blocks down the street. "The informant told us about the mutt. I got something that will shut it up."

"You're not hurting a dog on my watch."

Tamang patted a plastic shopping bag on the seat next to him.

"I got a steak here laced with a sleeping drug."

"I thought Hindus don't eat beef."

"Dogs aren't Hindus, dumbass. Unless he was a really bad Hindu and got reincarnated as a dog."

"What are you going to be reincarnated as?"

"I shudder to think. Hope that stuff doesn't turn out to be true. Let me go around the block and toss this to Rover. Stay here. You stand out here too much, white boy."

"Right."

Tamang turned off the lights and let the engine idle. When he left, Jacob slid into the driver's seat and pulled out a pair of binoculars.

Focusing them on the house, he could see the narrow, three-story concrete structure had all its shutters closed and a bright exterior light shining on the front door. He couldn't make out if there was a security camera. Hopefully, they put enough faith in that dog to warn them of any prowlers. That dog sure liked to bark.

Liked it too much. That made it unreliable as a watchdog. The Communists had probably gotten so sick of its yapping they didn't pay much attention anymore.

Arjun strolled down the dimly lit street with the shopping bag, looking like any other resident making his weary way home. He was still a block away when the dog ran to the length of its chain and started barking at him. Without breaking stride, Tamang reached into the bag, pulled out the steak, tossed it onto the lawn, and kept on going.

The dog pounced on it and stopped barking.

Tamang strolled past the house, made a right turn, came around the block, and got back in the car with Jacob.

"Nice work, Arjun. Nobody looked out the windows."

"Now we just got to wait. Let's get on our gear."

The two men struggled into their Kevlar vests and helmets within the cramped interior of the car, elbowing each other and cursing. Once finished, Jacob looked through the binoculars again.

No one was at any of the windows. The dog stood listlessly in the middle of the lawn. After a minute, it curled up and appeared to go to sleep.

"Nice work," Jacob said.

"It should be out for a couple of hours."

Jacob checked the car clock. It had just passed midnight.

"Let's go."

Without turning on the lights, they drove to the opposite side of the street from the safe house and parked. Then they looked around, saw the coast was clear, and got out. Jacob carried his usual MP5 submachinegun and a 9mm pistol, while Tamang had a heavier M4 carbine assault rifle and a 9mm. Each man had three stun grenades. The plan was to get captives, not a body count.

Spacing themselves widely apart, they sprinted for the front door.

They got to the door without any reaction coming from inside the house. No security camera in sight. As Tamang provided cover and glanced all around to make sure they weren't seen, Jacob got to work on the lock with a set of lockpicks. The lock was a simple one, and he got it in less than thirty seconds. Stowing his lockpicks, he readied his submachine gun, turned on the pen flashlight clipped beneath the barrel, and grabbed the door handle, hoping there wasn't a bolt on the inside. Kicking the door down would wake everyone up.

He eased the door open.

No bolt, but there was a burglar alarm.

No visible wires, no stickers to warn potential burglars, but a hidden burglar alarm for just such an occasion as this.

A shrill beeping daggered his eardrums.

Shouting a curse he could barely hear, they rushed inside.

The bottom floor, they knew from the schematic, was given over to a living room, kitchen, and bathroom. Agent Tamang positioned himself at the bottom of the stairs, aiming upstairs. Jacob rushed through the living room, scanning with his flashlight, kicked the door open on the bathroom, saw no one, and moved into the kitchen.

Just as he did, the thud of a stun grenade shook the building. Tamang must have thrown one upstairs at someone responding to the alarm.

No one on the ground floor. He hadn't expected there to be but there was no way he was going upstairs and putting his back to any potential danger.

He rushed back to find Tamang still at the bottom of the stairs waiting for him. Once he rejoined him, the Nepalese-American headed up, taking the lead. Through ringing ears, Jacob could hear shouts and running feet.

They took the stairs three at a time. At the top lay a man in pajamas flat out unconscious. His appearance was probably what prompted Tamang to toss the grenade.

Past the landing was a short hall and four doors. Two were open. In the doorway lay a man who was just trying to get to his hands and knees. A swift blow to the head with the butt of Tamang's assault rifle put him back down.

Jacob kicked in the nearest closed door and blinked as the light in the room suddenly came on.

A man stood there with a snarl on his face and a pistol in his hand.

A pistol aimed right at Jacob.

CHAPTER THIRTEEN

Jacob and the Communists fired at the same moment. Jacob felt an impact that felt like a sledgehammer to his chest, and he flew back into the hallway, banging against the far wall. The Communist, arms cartwheeling, flew back as well, hit the bedside table, and toppled sideways to the ground.

Jacob staggered for a moment, managed to keep on his feet, and raised his MP5 again. The wounded man, a bloodstain spreading on the side of his shirt, fumbled and picked up his weapon from where he had dropped it.

A short burst took care of him.

Arjun Tamang was already kicking in the other closed door. Finding nothing, he turned to the stairway leading up to the third and final floor. The lights were on up there.

At least I didn't freeze this time, Jacob thought, following him as a dull pain grew in his chest. Jacob forced himself to ignore it.

Tamang peeked around the corner and ducked back immediately as a burst of fire missed him by a hair's breadth and stitched a line of holes in the back wall.

The Nepalese-American CIA agent pulled out another flash-bang grenade. Jacob got on his knees, making the pain in his chest double in intensity, and edged toward the corner of the stairway.

Tamang silently enunciated, "One … two … THREE … "

At the same moment, the two men peeked around the corner, Jacob to fire a long burst that tore up the upper landing, and Tamang to toss a grenade up there.

They ducked back an instant before the grenade went off.

Jacob was on his feet and running while the house was still shaking from the detonation.

He hadn't made it halfway up before he had to duck. A hand reached around with a pistol and unloaded blindly down the stairwell.

Jacob fired a burst as he fell, missed, and the hand withdrew.

He glanced over his shoulder and saw Tamang lying prone back at the bottom of the stairs. He wasn't moving.

Jacob flew down the stairs, turned and fired a burst back up to keep the terrorists out of sight, then grabbed Tamang by an equipment strap and hauled him out of the line of fire.

Worried that the Nepalese Communists might start tossing grenades of their own, he dragged Tamang further away and into one of the bedrooms.

For a moment, he paused as a wave of pain and nausea threatened to engulf him. Damn. Had he cracked a rib?

Quit whining. Arjun is way worse off than you.

He gave his colleague a quick look over and didn't see any wounds or blood, then he noticed the dent in the front of his helmet. Jacob glanced out the doorway to make sure he was still alone—the ringing in his ears from two stun grenades had basically made him deaf—and then gently unstrapped Tamang's helmet and eased it off.

A bump the size of a golf ball, oozing blood, was right in the center of his forehead.

Concussion? Worse? At least he was still breathing.

Nothing more he could do for him now. Jacob snapped a new magazine into his MP5 and peeked out of the room. Nothing. The guy Tamang had clubbed with his weapon was still out cold.

That's one prisoner, Jacob thought with grim determination. *That means I don't have to get another if these guys keep acting ornery.*

He stepped over to the landing and swung around the corner, leading with his gun …

… just as a terrorist did the same thing.

Jacob swung his barrel up to hit the longer barrel of the man's Kalashnikov, and a three-round burst chewed up the ceiling. As powdered concrete rained on them, they both lowered their guns to fire.

Jacob won. His was the shorter weapon, he stood below the man, and the terrorist's AK-47 had been knocked up a bit further than Jacob had raised his own weapon.

Sometimes j, just half a second, a tiny little variable, meant the difference between life and death.

A burst from Jacob's weapon took off the top of the man's head. Jacob continued firing to ravage the chest of the man coming down the stairs behind him. A third Communist at the top of the stairs leapt out of sight before Jacob could hit him.

Jacob struggled past the two falling bodies and then hesitated at the top of the stairs. Smoke was filling the upper landing, backlit by flames licking at the carpeting at the top of the stairs. Flash bang grenades had a bad habit of setting fires when used indoors.

Did he dare go around the corner? The guy was probably there. He stared down the barrel of his gun, waiting for the man to show himself. Maybe he should stay put.

But if he stayed put, that smoke and fire would get worse, obscuring his vision and perhaps making him cough or blink at a critical moment. His lungs and eyes already stung.

And there was the possibility of a grenade getting lobbed around that corner.

He could lob one of his own, but the layout of the upper floor gave the guy plenty of shelter. Plus, it would mean unreadying his weapon for a full two seconds. Firefights had hinged on far less time than that.

Weighing all these factors took less than a second in Jacob's mind, and he came to a decision.

If in doubt, go forward. Good life advice no matter what you're facing.

He swung low around the corner, firing as he went, and ended up shooting nothing but air.

The light was on in the hallway, and two doors facing each other on either side of the hallway were closed, no light coming from within. A glass door led to a porch at the far end of the hallway. No one was visible beyond but with no light on out there it was hard to tell, plus there were blind spots to either side of the glass door.

Wonderful.

He saw the trap immediately. The guy was either lying in wait in one of the rooms, watching for Jacob's shadow to darken the slit of light shining beneath the door, or he was out on the porch, waiting for Jacob's shadow to become visible on the hallway floor.

Jacob decided the best way to handle this was to get back onto the landing and toss another stun grenade. The force would crack that glass door and with luck fling the other two doors open.

Just as Jacob decided this, the light to his right grew bright. The flames on the carpet had whooshed up and now blocked the entire landing. Smoke, already curling along the ceiling, began to thicken and lower.

Why me?

Jacob got prone, the smoke already tickling his nostrils and stinging his eyes. The thin air and the hyperventilation brought on by combat made him dizzy with too little oxygen, and him breathing too much was only sucking more smoke into his lungs. He coughed loudly, felt a jab of pain like a knife piercing him, suppressed another cough, and then coughed some more. That phantom knife got really stabbed.

I should have waited downstairs and smoked the bastard out.

Looks like the only way is forward now.

He leopard crawled, knees and elbows, to just ahead of the doors, taking care that his shadow would not be visible through the bottom cracks. Then he rose, reached over, and sent a burst through the lefthand one, arcing down to hit anyone lying on the floor.

Nice idea, but the guy turned out to be behind the righthand door.

Jacob's MP5 flew from his hands as a bullet struck it.

He was backpedaling and drawing his sidearm as the door opened and the Communist came out gripping his AK-47.

Jacob had just enough time to flick off the safety and take him out, then advance and keep firing, because no one with both his hands on an assault rifle could open a door.

He winged the second man just as he flew out of sight and kept on passing along the hall to get a better view.

Jacob caught his target as he tried to hide in the far corner of the darkened room. A bullet to the chest and another to the head as he fell took out that threat.

Jacob cleared the room, grabbed the man's AK-47 and, coughing and blinking, fired a burst through the glass door. Once he had made a hole, he ducked back inside the room, readied a flash bang, and tossed it through the opening into the porch.

He had just enough time to get out of the way before the flash bang sent a hailstorm of glass down the corridor.

Jacob rushed out on to the porch and found he had wasted a grenade. There was no one out here.

Faces stared out of windows all around the neighborhood. The flashing lights of a distance police car drew closer.

Jacob went back inside and saw the flames had spread.

He went back onto the porch and looked down. Too far to jump without risking his ankles. He had to get down there, though, and pull Tamang out before the flames spread downstairs.

Hurrying back to the bedroom, he tore the sheets off the bed and twisted them up into a cord, tying off both ends to keep it tight.

By the time Jacob emerged into the hallway, coughing his lungs out and getting eviscerated by that phantom knife-wielding maniac, he was surprised to see the flames had gone down a bit. After a moment, the glow went down even further, accompanied by a puff of smoke.

Curious, he moved over to the landing, squatting low and holding his breath, to find most of the flames gone.

Through a haze of smoke, he saw Tamang run up the stairs with a bucket of water in his hands.

"You all right?" Jacob asked, then coughed.

"Got knocked out for a bit," Tamang said, coughing too. "I got a hell of a headache and I'm pretty unsteady on my feet, but I'll be fine. Are you always this much of a disaster?"

"Sometimes I'm worse," he replied. "Just ask Jana."

CHAPTER FOURTEEN

The next morning, Jana sat in Professor Mahesh Bishwakarma's cluttered office while the professor and Prakash Rai had a loud argument in Nepali. They had been having it for a while, ever since Jana had brought up the *cyar mey* symbol and Prakash had shared his theories.

Jana didn't understand a word but she understood everything, because she had witnessed or been involved in this kind of argument dozens of times before.

Prakash was unloading his theories with all the enthusiasm of a true believer while Professor Bishwakarma got increasingly frustrated when the antiques dealer discounted every established academic fact he used as a counterargument.

They were, to put it briefly, getting nowhere. And they would continue getting nowhere all day unless Jana put a stop to it.

Jana raised her hands and cried out, "Enough! Whoever stole the Royal Vajra and whoever slaughtered the archaeological field crew obviously thinks the *cyar mey* is important. Can we just focus on that, please?"

The two Nepalese stared at her, struggling between traditional Asian hospitality and the typical male dislike of being shouted down by a woman.

Jana pointed to the photo on the dead archaeologist's phone, a photo that showed the missing stone from the temple wall.

On it was painted the *car mey* above a colorfully painted landscape of mountains and a valley filled with a village. Some writing was next to it, but an Anglo woman crouched in front of it, smiling at the camera while pointing at the symbol.

The two men calmed down and examined the photo once again, either out of Asian hospitality or scholarly interest she wasn't sure.

It didn't matter. The mission mattered, and she had to keep these two guys focused.

"It is a most peculiar drawing," Professor Bishwakarma said as if he was conceding a point.

"It's as clear as day," Prakash Rai declared. "It's the *cyar mey* powering a city."

"That's not a city, that's a village."

"Villages don't fill entire valleys."

"That's just artistic license. There were no cities in the uplands of the Himalayas until the nineteenth century."

"Can you puzzle out what the writing is?" Jana asked, heading off another argument.

Both men shook their heads.

"We can't see enough," the professor said.

"What about these other images?" Jana asked.

She switched from the dead archaeologist's phone to her own. The dead person's phone, while it had many images of the dig, didn't have an entire catalog of every painted image on the interior of the monastery walls. Jana had gone around and made sure she captured them all.

Jana slowly went through them. Some were blocks of texts, mostly incomplete because of the missing upper courses of stone. Others were images of Buddhas and various symbols she didn't recognize.

Jana and the two Nepalese scholars winced as she came to a photo of a beautifully painted Buddha. Lying in the dirt in the background was a Nepalese worker, his clothes soaked in blood.

"These are remarkable paintings," the professor said at last. "They remind me of the style of the Order of the Sacred Lotus."

Prakash Rai nodded in agreement and explained, "The Order of the Sacred Lotus is a monastic order stretching back centuries. They have a long artistic tradition of painting on the walls of their monasteries in this very style. Most monastic orders decorate their monasteries with silk wall hangings or tapestries. This order is one of ascetics. They feel such things are too worldly and distract from the pursuit of enlightenment."

"Then why the paintings? Aren't those worldly?"

Both Nepalese laughed. "This is Tibetan Buddhism, not Zen Buddhism. The symbolism is sacred and instructive. It's the silk and gold that's worldly."

"Oh, of course," Jana said, blushing. She felt very much out of her depth. This wasn't her area of specialty at all.

Tyler Wallace had fallen for the typical assumption of the public that any archaeologist knew about all periods and all regions. Nothing could be further from the truth. Most archaeologists were hyperspecialized. Many of her colleagues had criticized her as being a "generalist" for studying the Roman Empire as a whole, refusing to get bogged down in the minutiae of pottery seriation or regional trade routes like so many specialists.

She preferred being a generalist. While she couldn't claim to be the world's number one authority on some obscure aspect of the past, she did get to see the larger picture.

But she wasn't enough of a generalist to know about this stuff.

"The texts are typical prayers and extracts from various sacred books," the professor explained. "The symbol of the *car key* is the only thing that's truly unusual."

"That and the fact that it's powering a city," Prakash added.

Professor Bishwakarma muttered something under his breath.

"Would the Order of the Sacred Lotus know what the accompanying text was?" Jana asked. "I know this particular monastery was abandoned several hundred years ago, but you said they had a long and enduring tradition. Perhaps they used this particular arrangement of text and image regularly."

The professor scratched his head. "Well, the order is a shadow of its former self. Like all human institutions, it waxes and then wanes. I believe there is only one functioning monastery left."

He looked to Prakash for affirmation, and the antiquities dealer nodded. Jana felt reassured that these two were cooperating despite their differences. The series of crimes must have made them fear for their country's future.

It sure made Jana worry.

"So where is this monastery?"

"In the far northwest of the country," the professor answered, "in a little valley between the peaks near the border with both India and China."

"Wonderful," Jana said with a sigh. "The whole region is going to be crawling with troops. I'm not sure we'll be able to get up there."

"You must try if you're going to solve this," the professor said. Once again, Prakash nodded in agreement.

"And you should keep an open mind when they give you their answer," the antiquities dealer added.

***

In a dark, dingy basement in the prison of Kathmandu's army base, their prisoner was not looking pretty.

A military "interrogation expert", a hulking fellow stripped to the waist, had been using what he called "persuasion techniques" on the Communist.

Those persuasion techniques mainly consisted of beating the crap out of him.

Jacob did not like torture, and he did not like torturers. Beating a man to a pulp in a fair fight was one thing; doing it while he was strapped to a chair was another.

Plus, it didn't even work all that well. The subject might put on a brave face, as this one had, but eventually they'd crack and tell you whatever they thought you wanted to hear.

Jacob didn't want to hear what he wanted to hear. He wanted to hear the truth.

So far, the subject had claimed over and over that the Nepalese People's Liberation Front had nothing to do with the theft of the Royal Vajra or the attacks on the border post or archaeology dig.

Jacob wasn't sure if he believed him or not. The Nepalese army had cracked their cell phones easily enough and found a lot of communications, none of them related to any of those three operations.

Of course, like many insurgencies, the Nepalese People's Liberation Front operated in a cell structure. One cell knew little or nothing about the operations or identities of the other cells. Better security that way.

At least he and Tamang hadn't gotten into trouble for what they did. As his colleague had predicted, they were grateful for the help, although they would tell the press the operations had been conducted by the Nepalese military.

Fair enough. There was even discussion of their getting medals.

Jacob didn't want a medal. He just wanted to go home.

He also wanted the pain in his chest to stop. No cracked ribs, just the mother of all bruises.

Bad enough.

As a meaty fist thumped against the terrorist's swollen face for the umpteenth time, Jacob figured the odds. The Communists couldn't have too many cells in Kathmandu, so the chances that this one wasn't involved seemed slim. Also, the informant, now the proud owner of a ticket out of Nepal and a Green Card, insisted that he had heard nothing about the group perpetrating any of these crimes. Of course, this came out after he got his reward, not before. He had wanted to keep his offer as juicy as possible.

The Communist cried out, then gave a long monologue. One of the officers standing nearby spoke decent English and translated.

"He's challenging us. He asks why the Nepalese People's Liberation Front would steal a religious object when religion is the opium of the people. He says they have no interest in such a thing."

That fact had been bothering Jacob for some time now. The terrorists who took the Royal Vajra had said they were taking it so it "will be an object of power for the people." Jacob had assumed that meant a show of force by the Communists, but perhaps they meant a religious power. That jived with the other part of their statement saying it was wasted in the royal palace and the museum.

The Communist spat out some blood onto the boot of the interrogator, got a slap in return, and went on. The officer translated.

"He also asks why they would attack the border post if it wasn't to assist an invasion, and why they would gun down a bunch of archaeologists who weren't oppressing the people. The Nepalese People's Liberation Front has no interest in the past, he states, only in the future."

Jacob looked at the officer. "He's got a point."

The officer scowled at the prisoner. "They must have done it. Who else would?"

"Damn good question," Jacob muttered. He excused himself. He needed some air. The sound of a fist hitting flesh followed him as he walked down the corridor and up into the military base, accompanied by a soldier as a guide.

Torture bothered him. It rarely worked and was more for the gratification of the captors than for learning any valuable intel. He knew enough to know that he wouldn't be able to stop it in this case, however. That Communist operative was in for a long day.

God, I'm getting tired of this crap.

As soon as he got out into the fresh air, he took a deep breath and called Jana.

He glanced at the soldier. While the young guy had indicated he spoke no English, Jacob wasn't fooled. He'd been assigned to the foreigner because he could listen in.

Fine. Let him listen in. Jacob was beginning not to care.

Jana picked up. "How are things with the prisoner?"

"Not getting anywhere. I don't think the Commies did it. They don't really have a reason to and we found no evidence in their safe house."

"You sound upset."

He glanced at the soldier again, who was staring off into space.

"Just tired. And you?"

"I think I have a lead, but we'll need permission to go to a sensitive border area to speak to some Buddhist monks."

"That would be a nice change of pace over our usual company."

"So who do you think did it?" Jana asked.

"I don't know."

"You free to talk?"

"Not really."

"Do you think it's our old professor friend?"

"It might be." Professor Harlow had the interest and the ruthlessness.

"We'll talk later. Come on back to the hotel."

Those were the best words he'd heard all day. He wanted to lie in bed with her and not come out for a week.

CHAPTER FIFTEEN

"I was wondering when you were going to show up," Jana grumbled.

A man stood at the entrance to her hotel.

He was tall, easily six-four, with a lanky build, a deeply tanned face from long hours in the sun, and salt and pepper hair swept back in a rather affected style. He wore a conservative tailored suit, the jacket of which hung a bit loosely on his frame.

She knew that hid a shoulder holster, because she knew who this was.

Robert Bledshaw, director of the Antiquities Division. He had the knowledge of a university professor and the combat skills of a Green Beret.

And the transparency of the IRS.

Bledshaw bowed, and in a refined accent that spoke of boarding school and the Ivy League, he said, "I'm thrilled to see you again, Jana. Are you glad to see me?"

"It depends. Why are you here?" She glanced to the left and right to make sure no one was close, and in a lower voice said, "Is Dr. Harlow behind this?"

"I think it best that we speak in the privacy of your hotel room. Jacob is already up there."

Of course, you'd know that.

"I'm sure he'll be delighted to see you," Jana grumbled.

"I do look forward to our reunion," he said with a cheery air.

They entered the hotel and ascended the steps as Bledshaw made small talk about the sights in Kathmandu. Jana didn't ask any of the million questions she had. Jacob would want to know the answers too.

Jana knocked at the door. Quicker than she expected, Jacob unlocked and opened it.

"Hey honey, I'm so glad … oh."

"Good afternoon, Agent Snow." Again, that irritating bow. "May I come in?"

"Damn right, you can come in," Jacob snarled. "You have some explaining to do."

They entered, Jacob slammed and locked the door behind them, and they all sat down, Jacob glaring at the newcomer.

"What have you discovered in your investigations so far?" Robert Bledshaw asked.

"No way," Jana grunted. "You first."

Bledshaw gave a little shrug and said, "Very well. When we heard about the theft of the Royal Vajra, we became concerned that Professor Harlow is up to his old tricks again."

"It seems like a reasonable hypothesis," Jana said. "Do you have any hard evidence?"

"No."

"Neither do we. What took you so long to get here? We've been here for two days."

"We had some other matters to attend to."

"Like what?"

"Just other matters."

Here we go again.

"What do you know about the Royal Vajra?" Jacob asked, showing the irritation Jana was trying to hide.

"That it's a holy relic of great cultural and religious importance to all the Himalayan peoples."

Jana clicked her tongue. "Come on. There's more than that. You wouldn't show up in Paris if the Mona Lisa was stolen."

Robert Bledshaw smiled. "Saying that proves you don't know much about the Mona Lisa."

Jana ignored that and persisted. "What do you know about the Royal Vajra that makes it important to the Antiquities Division?"

"I'd like to help you, but I'm not in a position to offer any more information unless you are willing to collaborate."

Jana and Jacob traded a look.

"Could you leave us for a minute?" she asked.

Bledshaw nodded, rose, and walked into the hallway. Jana gave him a hard stare and he walked a little way down the hallway.

Jana still stared at him. He gave her another of his annoying little bows and said, "I'll wait on the street outside."

Then he left.

Jana closed the door and the two of them went to the window. After a moment, Bledshaw appeared and stepped over to the other side of the street, where he stood watching the passersby.

Even so, Jana turned the TV on loud just in case. They had both learned never to underestimate this man.

"What do you think?" Jana asked, keeping her voice down.

"I don't trust him."

"He didn't turn out so bad in the last mission," Jana pointed out.

"He did what he had to do. What does he have to do now? We don't know what he's been up to these last few months except for a few brief phone calls that told us nothing except that he was still alive."

In gratitude for Bledshaw unmasking his boss, the Curator, who Bledshaw was under orders not to even acknowledge the existence of, Jacob and Jana had told him in front of the crew of goons that had come to pick him up and take him back to base that he should call regularly to show them that he was still alive.

An implied threat to the Antiquities Division, except they had no idea if they could follow through. They didn't know where the Curator was based, and it was a U.S. government institution so they're hands were pretty much tied anyway.

Still, the calls had come, and Bledshaw was still breathing. But in those calls, he talked of nothing of importance and said goodbye after only a couple of minutes.

So they knew nothing of his current relationship with the Curator, or whether he was still director, or anything about what he had been up to in the past few months.

Jana and Jacob thought for a moment. On the TV, a Nepalese journalist was speaking from a news desk. The scene cut to a general at a podium making an angry speech and shaking his fist in the air.

"I think we need him," Jana said.

"Well, he's involved in this whether we like it or not. I guess having him where we can keep an eye on him is the best course of action."

Jacob didn't sound too happy about that. Jana sure knew how he felt.

"So I guess the question is, how much do we reveal to him?" Jana said.

"He's obviously here because of that *cyar mey* symbol and its connection to ancient power for that old civilization." Jacob raised a hand before she could point out the scientific implausibility of that statement. "He believes it, and Professor Harlow believes it. That's what matters."

Jana couldn't argue with that. Just like when she'd tangled with terrorists, she was once again having to deal with irrational people who would stop at nothing to further their crazy beliefs. But unlike with the terrorists, there was no clear demarcation between good and evil. While Dr. Harlow had killed tens of thousands of people to unmask the Curator, the Curator had let it happen by refusing to give himself up. They had been stuck in the case until Bledshaw had admitted the Curator was a real person and arranged an interview.

So Bledshaw's better nature could be trusted to a point. His boss, on the other hand, couldn't be trusted at all.

Jana considered for a moment. "He's obviously reached out to us because he thinks we know things he doesn't, and I'm sure he knows lots we don't. I think we should work with him. Let's tell him everything. At the moment, that's not much."

Jacob looked uncomfortable. "Everything? I suppose. But he better give something back. And let's not name our informants. I don't want the Antiquities Division harassing them. Who knows what they're capable of."

"Agreed. And Professor Harlow might still have moles in the organization. It might be dangerous to give Bledshaw names."

They went to the window and motioned for him to return. As Jana went to turn off the TV, the news program was showing Nepali troops high in a mountain unloading equipment.

We better solve this before it escalates out of control, Jana thought. *Assuming it hasn't already.*

Bledshaw sat down with them and they told him all they had learned. He must have noted the lack of names provided, but he did not comment on this.

After they finished, he spoke.

"I agree that it wasn't this Communist group who did all or even any of the attacks. It doesn't make sense, as you say. I think it was Professor Harlow. He wants to tap the power of the *cyar mey* and stealing the Royal Vajra is a good first step."

"What do you know about this power?" Jacob asked. Jana tried to control her impatience.

"There are many legends about how Civilization X got its power."

"Civilization X?" Jana asked.

"That's what we call the civilization from a hundred thousand years ago, since we don't know what they called themselves."

"You never called it that on our last mission."

"Our research has advanced since then," he said with a dismissive gesture. "In any case, Civilization X obviously had extensive power needs, given that they had lighting, large cities, and similar modes of transport to our own. Where did they get the electricity? If you sample ice cores, you can trace the emission of carbon from sources such as coal and oil. No such emissions have been found from such an early date. We would expect at least as much as you see from ice cores dating to the Industrial Revolution, and yet we find nothing."

That's because there's nothing to find, Jana thought. She kept that to herself. They had gotten Bledshaw talking, and that was such a rare occurrence that she didn't want to interrupt.

Bledshaw went on.

"So how did they power highly advanced cities without carbon emissions? Photovoltaics? Hydroelectric dams? Nuclear fission or fusion? Possible, but we've found no evidence of that. We believe it could have been some different power source, something unknown to our science."

"The *car mey*," Jacob said.

"Exactly. This is a new line of research for us. I'm afraid we've spent too much time on the more accessible regions of study, such as India and North Africa, where Civilization X had outposts. Their main areas of population got erased by the Ice Age, so we've been put in the odd situation of trying to study a civilization through its outposts. Until now, we haven't spent nearly enough time on the most remote of those outposts, those located high in the Himalayas. It's a sensitive region, after all, and we don't have access to a large portion of it thanks to the intransigence of the Chinese government."

"What changed your attitude?" Jana asked.

"The Royal Vajra being displayed in public. Until then, we'd never gotten a good look at it. The royal family had never published photos of it. All we had were some simple drawings by an eighteenth-century British traveler, and we weren't sure those were accurate. When the press release for the grand opening of the Himalayan Heritage Museum came out, we were astonished to see the capabilities of the artifact."

"What capabilities?" Jana asked. "It's just a really big vajra."

Bradshaw shook his head. "You have it the wrong way around. The vajras of Nepalese tradition, and the identical dorje of Tibetan tradition, are in fact miniature models. Imitations by later cultures who understood its importance but not its true power. The Royal Vajra is the real thing, perhaps the only surviving example."

"Of what?"

"A power conduit for the *car mey*." Bledshaw held up a silencing hand. "We think. Our research is still lacking in this aspect."

Jacob rubbed his jaw. "So you think Professor Harlow stole the Royal Vajra in order to tap into the *cyar mey* and use it?"

Jana groaned. Bledshaw ignored her and said, "Perhaps. We're still too early in our studies to be sure."

"Use it for what?" Jacob asked.

"Again, we don't know. I'm sure you'll agree, however, that if Dr. Harlow wants it, we don't want him to have it."

"So you want to team up with us?" Jacob asked. "What do you bring to the table?"

"Resources. Connections. I can get you to that monastery."

"You can convince the Nepalese government to allow three foreigners, two of whom are in the CIA, to go to a sensitive border area when they're on the brink of war?"

Bledshaw smiled. "They'll even pack us a picnic lunch."

Jacob smiled back at him. "Looks like you're going to be useful."

Looks like we're getting played, Jana thought.

CHAPTER SIXTEEN

Jacob breathed in the sharp mountain air and soaked up the matchless beauty of his surroundings.

The village of Aaru Kunde lay nestled in a narrow, sloping valley fringed with jagged peaks of black stone. Beyond these rose higher peaks capped with snow that gleamed painfully in the sun in vivid contrast to the lower black summits.

The village, a collection of a couple of hundred stone huts with slate roofs, stood on either side of a sparkling mountain stream that ran right down the center. A few Sherpas moved between the houses on various tasks. One man, who couldn't have been more than five-two, walked up the path with a bundle of firewood on his back that was almost as big as he was, held only by a burlap sack and a strap around his forehead.

Jacob stared in amazement. He couldn't have carried that more than a hundred yards in this altitude. They were just shy of 3000 meters here, and even though he had acclimatized to Kathmandu's altitude, they had just doubled it.

They had arrived by private helicopter from Kathmandu, cleared by the Nepalese military after a single call from Bledshaw.

The director of the Antiquities Division had been good to his word. So far.

Jacob strolled down a path with Jana, Bledshaw, and Agent Arjun Tamang, who had recovered from his injury and now wore a bandage wrapped around his head that made his hat look lumpy. Jacob had told his colleague that Bledshaw was with the U.S. Antiquities Division and was a federal agent. Tamang, of course, had never heard of this agency and asked a million questions. Jacob told him what he needed to know—that the Antiquities Division and its nemesis Dr. Harlow both sought artifacts from an advanced prehistoric civilization. He left out the details about the scummy dealings within the Antiquities Division. Jacob regretted not telling him more, but he was already breaching classified material. He justified that as necessary for the mission.

Jacob also regretted having to leave Detective Gurung back in the capital. The guy was more spiritual than Tamang and his insight would have been useful, but with the theft and the mass murder investigation, the Nepalese police force needed every man on the job.

That also signaled a disturbing shift in the government's attitude. This was no longer a police matter, but an army one.

And the army had sent a minder.

To avoid attracting more attention than they already would, the helicopter had flown into a neighboring valley, where they were met by a compact young corporal who drove them in a Hummer over to the village. Like the sentry back at the army base who had followed Jacob around, Corporal Koirala claimed not to speak any English.

Jacob wasn't fooled. Any time they were talking, Corporal Koirala kept close and kept quiet.

Still, the relative lack of oversight by the Nepalese army was surprising. Three foreigners, and one half foreigner, were being left pretty much to their own devices.

Why?

They walked up a steep path cut into the rock near the edge of the stream, heading for the village. The army had geared them up with hooded parkas and warm leggings, plus thick hats and gloves made of yak wool. Trekking glasses, with dark lenses and shades on the sides, preserved their eyes from the glare of the snow. Even bundled up like this, Jacob felt a chill every time they stopped to rest, which was far too often. While neither he or Jana were experiencing headaches or confusion or any other severe symptoms of altitude sickness, they got tired much more easily than normal. He hoped there wouldn't be any running involved in this part of the mission.

Robert Bledshaw seemed just fine. Jacob eyed him. Had he been in high altitudes for a while now? Here in the Himalayas? If so, what had he been up to?

Jacob dismissed that question as unknowable. It wasn't like Bradshaw was going to share that information.

The valley took a slight turn, and Jacob's breath caught.

Not from the altitude, at least not this time, but from the stunning sight ahead of them.

The sloping valley ascended more steeply past the village, angling a bit to the east. Now that they were further into the valley, they could see all the way to the back, where the valley opened onto a steep slope where snow had gathered in the shaded declivities. High above the valley floor, clinging to the side like barnacles, were a series of wooden red-columned buildings with pagoda-style roofs. It was an extensive network of buildings that Jacob estimated could easily hold a hundred people.

The monastery of the Order of the Sacred Lotus.

"Impressive, isn't it?" Agent Tamang said.

Jacob only nodded.

Corporal Koirala said a few words, and Tamang translated.

"He says the military asked the mayor of Aaru Kunde to speak with the abbot. At first the abbot was hesitant to meet with a bunch of foreigners, but given the situation he agreed."

"Well, you're not a foreigner."

"I'm a half foreigner," Tamang said, "plus I'm Hindu, not Buddhist."

"And our young friend the corporal?"

"He's Buddhist."

"Good."

They walked through the village, getting a lot of stares. The bolder among the children peppered Agent Tamang and Corporal Koirala with questions. Jana smiled and waved. Jacob saved his energy. His chest still hurt from that his Kevlar took.

By the time they had passed through the village, they had a small crowd of children following them. Just past the last of the houses stood a small, older Sherpa man waiting for them and holding several white scarves. He spoke. As Tamang translated, he put a scarf around each of the newcomers and greeted them.

Jana put her hands together and bowed her head. Jacob took her cue and did the same.

"This is Pasang Lobsang Sherpa, the mayor of Aaru Kunde. He greets us all and thanks us for coming all this way to help retrieve the Royal Vajra."

"The military told him our mission?" Bradshaw asked, obviously unhappy with this revelation. "I can understand telling the abbot, but this man—"

Tamang cut him off. "This man got us an audience with the abbot. We needed a trusted outsider as a go-between."

"Very well," Bledshaw muttered.

"He'll lead us up to the monastery."

Jacob looked at the narrow steps cut into the steep stone slope and took a few deep breaths. He was going to need them.

They started to ascend. The children stayed at the edge of the village. Mayor Pasang Lobsang Sherpa went up those steps with the assurance of a mountain goat. He began to leave them behind until he glanced over his shoulder, saw the foreigners lagging, and stopped to wait. The faint sound of giggling came up from below. The children were watching.

"We're not making a very good impression on the locals," Jacob huffed.

"You want to race?" Tamang said in a cheerful voice. "Fifty bucks to the winner. I'll give you a ten-second head start."

"No thanks."

"Twenty seconds?"

"Shut up."

Jana laughed, then cut off quick and took a couple of deep breaths.

"You'll get accustomed to it after a few days," Bradshaw said.

A few days of doing what? Jacob wondered. *Seems like you've been here for a while.*

After what seemed like ages but was in fact probably only ten minutes, they took a break. The foreigners stood huffing and puffing, the white plumes of air from their mouths making them look like steam engines. Even Bledshaw looked a bit tired.

They clutched their scarves so the stiff breeze didn't snatch them off. Jacob figured that wouldn't be good symbolism.

Jacob looked up at the monastery, still high up ahead. There was a porch around the edge of the nearest building covered by a pagoda-style roof held up by red columns. No one appeared to be there, or at any of the windows he could see. He heard nothing—no prayers, no religious music, nothing.

Then he looked down at the valley below them and gasped.

The village nestled between the black peaks looked stunning, the vast range of mountains beyond it even more so. He could see for miles, and other than the village of Aaru Kunde, he saw no sign of human habitation.

"You have a beautiful country, Arjun."

"My country is the United States, but thank you. It's good to come back sometimes. Shall we continue?"

That got groans from all three foreigners. Arjun Tamang chuckled, said something to the mayor and the corporal, and they continued.

Up, up, up. Jacob concentrated on putting one foot in front of the other. His head began to ache. They must have ascended another 200 meters at least. Hopefully this mission wouldn't make them go any higher.

Of course it will, Jacob thought. *These missions always make me do something worse than I've done before. Maybe I'll write that resignation letter for real this time.*

And how would Jana take that? Would she keep going on missions alone or with some other partner?

You're stuck, buddy.

Damn.

They came to a ledge barely big enough for them all to stand huddled together. The mayor motioned for them to stop and through Tamang informed them that they had to leave their weapons here, as none were allowed in the monastery.

Everyone started unloading. Bledshaw hesitated for a moment, glanced up at the monastery, and took out a pistol that he laid on the smooth stone.

"The backup, too," Jacob told him.

"I was just getting to that."

Sure you were.

He pulled out a smaller, holdout pistol and set it down.

Once everyone had at least apparently divested themselves of weapons, they headed up.

Jacob didn't like going into an unknown place without any firearms or even a knife, but he had a feeling these monks could tell if he was carrying or not.

Besides, how dangerous could a Buddhist monastery be?

They huffed and puffed up the last length of stairs, the frigid wind biting every exposed bit of flesh, and at last came up to the landing. Ahead of them stood a long, single-story building, larger than it had looked from below.

Beyond the arcaded porch stood a large set of double doors that shone with black lacquer and a golden emblem that looked like stylized writing.

A clatter of a wooden bolt, and the doors opened with a creak.

Jacob had watched some videos of Buddhist monasteries in this region and they all looked like they followed the Tibetan tradition with long red robes, strange curved yellow hats, and loud ritual bands playing cymbals and long horns. The monks dressed in an ornamental fashion, each color and accoutrement a potent symbol of their religion.

That was not the case with the three monks who faced them. They wore simple red tunics and sandals that would have given Jacob hypothermia in two minutes. They stood erect, with eyes that took in everything.

Jacob's eyes took in everything too, especially the tight, muscular bodies, the easy poise, and the callouses on their knuckles.

These were warrior monks. Jacob didn't think they existed here. Then again, the professor back in Kathmandu had told Jana this was an ancient, isolated, and almost extinct order.

The two monks to either side pressed their hands together and bowed at the waist, making a perfect right angle with their bodies. The monk in the middle, older but no less fit, bowed slightly. Jacob figured this was not due to his age, but because of his rank. He looked like he was more fit than his younger brethren.

All the Nepalese in their group knelt and touched their heads to the ground.

Jacob bowed, but not that much. He'd show respect, but he would not show that much respect. He was a warrior too, after all.

Jana and Bledshaw both bowed deeper than he did.

One of the younger monks stepped forward, bowed again, and said in English,

"I am Prabal. We are honored by your visit. I will accompany and translate for you."

The older monk stepped forward and again they were each given white scarves. Jacob wished they were warmer. It was getting chilly standing up on this cliff face.

Thankfully, the three monks then led them inside and closed the doors behind them. Their breath still frosted the air, but at least they had shelter from the wind. The other young monk said something in Nepali and led the mayor and the corporal away down a bare corridor. The corporal hesitated for a moment, got a sharp look from the monk, and did as he was told.

He's probably disobeying an order right now and yet he didn't even object, Jacob thought. *Interesting. These monks have got a reputation.*

Prabal and the older monk led them down the opposite corridor, again bare of ornamentation. Jacob wondered where all these wall paintings were that Jana wanted to ask about. They passed a few closed doors, then took a right and went through a door back outside onto a small courtyard barely big enough to accommodate the dozen monks sitting in the lotus position on the bare stone, eyes half closed and serene.

Jacob stared. They wore the same simple robes as the others, their heads, hands, and feet bare. How could they not freeze to death?

Edging their way around these monks, who didn't move a muscle or an eye at the appearance of the strangers, they ascended some steps hacked into the steep slope and up to another building. There they came to an open porch and under the shade of the roof in a chair of lacquered wood sat an old man in yellow robes. His face was seamed with deep lines, but his eyes were sharp and clear as he studied each of the newcomers.

The two monks bowed deeply and motioned to cushions on the floor. Everyone sat cross-legged.

"The Esteemed Abbot greets you," Prabal said.

Everyone bowed. Jacob bowed deeper this time. If this guy was in charge of these warriors, he must have been a badass back in the day.

The abbot's eyes settled on him. Jacob held his gaze. He found it a difficult thing to do, there was force there, but he had a feeling he'd better. The sharp, cold wind blew through the open porch, the only sound.

The abbot said something, and the monk Prabal translated.

"The Esteemed Abbot says do not be ashamed to be a reluctant warrior, for that is the only good warrior there is."

Jacob blinked. What the hell?

The abbot turned to Jana and said through the translator, "True education expands constantly."

Jana looked confused.

Then he turned to Tamang and said something Prabal didn't translate. Tamang paled, sat up straighter, and gave a quick nod.

Then the abbot's gaze settled on Bledshaw. It remained there in silence for some time. To his credit, the director of the Antiquities Division managed to hold up under this scrutiny.

"If you clean out the pig's stall with your hands, you cannot complain of sickness when you bite your nails."

OK, now I'm really confused.

Bledshaw didn't exactly look enlightened either.

The abbot turned to look at Jacob again.

"You wish to know about the Royal Vajra and why someone would steal it. You are in hot pursuit of these criminals and thus I will be brief. The *cyar mey* was the greatest power of the Ancient Kingdom of Great Wisdom and Folly. Some say that it was used to power their cities and their amazing contrivances. It was indeed used for this, but it was more than that. It was also a weapon, the greatest weapon the world has ever known, far greater than the atomic bombs your nation inflicted on this world."

Jacob licked his lips and said, "An archaeological field crew was excavating an old monastery of your order a few hundred miles east of here and came across a painting of a vajra on the monastery's stone wall. Then some gunmen came and slaughtered every one of them and took all their photographic equipment. They also took the stone. One phone escaped their notice and that's how we know of their discovery. There was some writing next to it but that's not visible. We were wondering what that writing might signify."

"Let me see the photo."

Jana pulled out the phone and opened it to the photo. Prabal took it and showed it to the abbot.

Did Jacob sense an emotion in those placid features? Did his eyes widen a little, his lips open, his skin pale?

Before the abbot could speak, Jacob was distracted by something else.

A high, thin buzzing sound, growing louder.

He frowned and looked around. Where was that coming from? It was mechanical, not something he'd think to hear in this monastery at all. The monks were looking around too.

Then he realized what he was hearing.

Drones. A bunch of them.

CHAPTER SEVENTEEN

Jacob leapt up and whirled around just as three drones rose up into view about ten feet past the porch and cliff face. They had armor plating, and each had a machine gun slung beneath the main body. Beyond, he saw more killer attack drones spreading out over the monastery.

Each was equipped with a machine gun or a pair of small missiles.

"Run!" he shouted, grabbing Jana, who was already halfway to her feet.

The abbot sprang to his feet, picked up his heavy wooden throne as if it were paper, and tossed it at the center drone.

It smashed into the drone, and the machine plummeted out of sight.

The other two opened fire.

The bullets concentrated on the abbot and the two monks. All of them ducked and rolled out of the way as bullets chewed up the wall behind them.

"This way!" Prabal shouted, pointing to a doorway. He still held the phone with the image of the monastery painting.

Jacob didn't have time to admire the dexterity with which the monks had dodged the bullets. He was too busy running.

The machine guns sprayed the area. Tamang cried out and clamped a hand on his shoulder. Prabal flung the door open and the abbot disappeared through, Bledshaw right behind. The rest of them hurried through the portal.

Prabal made it. The other monk did not. He jerked and danced as a dozen bullets hit him, his red robes turning a deeper crimson.

Prabal slammed the door behind them.

"They'll hit us with a missile and come right in," Jacob told him. "We need to get deeper into the monastery."

Prabal nodded, and they ran down a corridor. They hadn't made it ten feet before a detonation threw them to the ground.

The door they had shut behind them shattered, flinging pieces of wood down the corridor. One large, flat piece struck Bledshaw in the back and flung him to the floor.

Prabal flung open a bureau standing nearby and revealed a rack of weapons—wooden staves, swords, spears, and polearms with various nasty-looking blades.

The monk grabbed a simple wooden staff and performed a cartwheel with it back down to the doorway just as a pair of drones buzzed through. With blinding speed, he swung his staff, knocked one straight into the stone floor with a crash, and then poked out the camera of the second, the glass shattering.

The second drone, although blinded, opened fire. Prabal's blow had turned it enough that its bullets did nothing but hit the wall.

The drone operator must have guessed this might happen because the drone did a 180, still firing. Everyone ducked to avoid the shots, which flew well overhead. Prabal launched himself up, hitting the bottom of the drone so it smashed against the ceiling, destroying its rotors and plunging to the ground. With two quick hits, he smashed the wiring of both drones.

"Get the Esteemed Abbot further inside!" he shouted. "He must not—"

The roar of a machine gun and Prabal's chest opened up in a gout of blood. He staggered for a moment and fell.

Another drone hovered just behind him. More were coming up fast.

Jacob glanced at Bledshaw. He wasn't moving.

No time to check. The lead drone was just closing in.

Then sparks flew off it and it spun up into the roof, its rotors shattering against a beam.

The abbot had thrown something. Jacob hadn't seen what.

Jana grabbed Bledshaw under both arms and dragged his limp body around the far corner of the hallway as the abbot took the lead. Tamang, still clutching his shoulder and panting, was the last person around and just made it to safety before a hail of bullets flew down the corridor.

The abbot threw open a door and motioned everyone inside.

They ended up in what looked like a training room. The floor was covered with thick carpeting, and on the walls were racks of weapons.

The abbot said something and motioned to the weapons. Jacob grabbed a polearm with a big, curved slicing blade that in medieval Europe had been called a glaive. He knew he looked foolish, but he felt better having something, anything in his hand. Jana dragged Bledshaw toward a far door.

"It would have been nice if we could have kept our guns," he told the abbot.

The abbot said something back that sounded mocking as he grabbed a pair of hand axes. Tamang grabbed a sword with a fancy red tassel hanging off the hilt.

"Jesus Christ, we're going to fight drones with martial arts?" Jacob cried. "Does no one else find this a really bad idea?"

"This is the second time you've led me into a disaster!" Tamang said.

"Get used to it," Jana called from the other side of the room. "Bledshaw's still breathing at least."

She reached for the door and yelped, jumping backwards as it flew open.

A dozen monks rushed in, calling out to the abbot and grabbing weapons off the racks.

Things are about to get weird, aren't they?

A blast blew the other door off its hinges. Everyone staggered back.

A missile drone hovered just beyond. With terrible clarity, Jacob saw that it had fired one to open the door and still had the other on its undercarriage.

A hailstorm of knives, shuriken, and spears battered the thing. Sparks flew from its wiring, a rotor got cut clean off, and it fell to the ground …

… only to be replaced with a pair of drones with machine guns.

They swooped in, heading straight for the abbot.

Just as they opened fire, a monk threw himself in front of the old man and took the bullets in his chest. More monks swarmed in to protect their leader. One monk, who looked more senior than the others, rushed in from the side and took out one of the drones with a flying kick.

The second drone turned and fired at him, chewing up the carpet as he rolled away.

Jacob rushed at it, swinging his glaive to hit the drone with a loud *clong*.

The drone spun out, recovered, and he hit the drone again.

That knocked it down enough that he could jab the tip of the glaive into the wiring near the top of the drone, twist, and snap several connections.

The drone went dead.

An explosion somewhere outside shook the building. Two more drones rounded the corner and turned toward them.

One carried a missile, the other a machine gun. Their operators, wherever they might be, had gotten wise and hung back out of reach. Jacob dodged to the right to get out of the line of fire.

To his surprise, none of the monks did. Instead, they sent a flurry of weapons at the two drones. Spears, shuriken, daggers, and darts flew at the killer machines. The abbot even threw one of his hand axes.

They concentrated on the one carrying the missile, which if it managed to fire could kill them all.

The abbot's hand ax crunched through the drone's outer plating. Jacob couldn't see if it was a killing blow because the next instant several more weapons hit it and it fell into half a dozen pieces.

The room filled with the roar of a machine gun as the other drone got into the fight. Several monks jerked and fell, the others springing out of the way.

Then the drone spun. Agent Tamang, blood streaming from his shoulder, had charged right for it, leapt up, and managed to hit the machine gun with the tip of his sword, sending the drone spinning around.

It did a 180 and trained its gun on the crowd once again.

A monk soared through the air and punched it. Jacob actually saw the metal plate buckle and the drone fly back a few feet before it trained its gun on the monk and took him out.

He was replaced the next moment by a monk with a staff, who smacked the drone hard, only to get his legs cut out from under him by the bullets.

A few other monks, having grabbed more weapons to throw, struck it with several knives and a spear. It wavered and lost altitude …

… bringing it close enough that Jacob could charge, swinging the glaive over his head to bring the heavy blade full force down on the rotors.

The little helicopter mechanism shattered, one blade slicing into Jacob's side, the rest flying in all directions to bang against the walls.

Jacob staggered, saw the drone now lying at his feet, and jabbed the glaive into the mechanism to disable it.

Glancing down the hallway, he saw another drone with a missile coming around the far corner.

"Run!" he shouted as he sprinted back into the training room.

At the far end of the room, Jana pulled Bledshaw out the door. While the monks couldn't understand Jacob's English, they sure understood his tone. Several of them pulled wounded comrades through the door behind Jana and Bledshaw, while others stood their ground, readying weapons they could throw.

A fatal mistake. Just before any of the rearguard could target the drone, it launched its miniature missile.

The explosion pushed Jacob out the door and into the courtyard outside, slamming into the abbot just ahead of him and throwing both of them to the ground.

For a moment, Jacob lay dazed. Then a pair of strong hands lifted him up and handed him back his glaive. Jacob blinked the dust out of his eyes and realized it was the abbot. Both of them looked back into the training room.

Bodies lay everywhere. The padded carpet was torn to shreds and smoldering in several spots. The racks of weapons lay in disarray on the floor.

The drone zipped through the wreckage after them. Jacob noted it didn't have any missiles left, but it did have its camera.

Watching them. Following them. Reporting back.

A hulking monk shouldered his way past and with a roar leapt into the air. The drone ascended to the ceiling but to no avail. The monk grabbed the landing gear, and his own weight pulled them back down to the floor. The monk swung it over his head and smashed it against a wall.

A moment later, he rolled back into the courtyard and bullets chewed up what remained of the carpet.

"Jesus! How many of these things are there?" Jacob cried.

"This way!" Jana shouted.

A monk had opened a portal into another building further up the slope. The courtyard was on a flattened stone ledge on the slope, a narrow set of stairs hewn into the rock leading to the next building. Smoke rose from some of the other buildings and they could hear the buzz of several drones. It was only a matter of moments before the drones found them.

And in this exposed position, the drones would cut them down with no problem.

They could hover out of range of anything the monks could throw and take them out.

Their only hope was to stay inside, where the limited space gave them their only advantage.

Everyone seemed to realize this at the same time and started running up the stairs. A monk helped Jana with Bledshaw. Tamang was still moving under his own power, but he didn't look like he could keep it up for long.

The abbot and some of the senior monks didn't even use the stairs, but sprinted up the smooth, angled stone like a herd of mountain goats.

Jacob huffed up the slope, the fresh cut in his side stinging, the bruise on his chest from the last fight aching, and his lungs burning from so much exertion at such an unaccustomed altitude.

I'm not going to be much good for long.

Gasping and dizzy, he was one of the last to the top of the steps. As people poured through the door to the hoped-for safety inside, Jacob turned and surveyed the scene.

Drones buzzed all around the monastery, firing missiles into the buildings or chasing monks caught outdoors, gunning them down as they tried to flee to safety.

This was a major operation, like something seen in a full-scale war. Only armies and large terrorist organizations had this many drones. No way the Nepalese People's Liberation Front could mount such an offensive. The Chinese could, but would they?

No, this must be Professor Harlow. He'd proven to have plenty of resources and no scruples.

Jacob scanned the mountains and nearby slopes for the drone operators. With dozens of drones, there had to be dozens of operators, a full military camp with heaps of high-tech gear. And they had to be more or less line-of-sight for their signals to get through.

The problem was, there were so many slopes and peaks overlooking this valley that they could be on any of them, even dozens of miles away.

They were helpless against the drone operators and almost helpless against the drones.

To his horror, all the drones in sight turned and started heading for their position.

The abbot was obviously the target, and one of those drones had spotted where he had fled. The operator back at base had alerted his colleagues and now they were all zeroing in on an old wooden building completely exposed on a mountain slope.

One of the monks grabbed him, pulled him in, and slammed the door.

The next moment, the drones started firing.

CHAPTER EIGHTEEN

Jana was getting sick of playing nursemaid to Robert Bledshaw while being chased by killer drones. Running from building to building was not going to keep them alive for long. It was time for a change of tactics.

But what?

They were in the front hallway of a building. Everyone raced through a set of double doors into an interior room just as a missile blew a big hole in an outside wall. Within a few seconds, drones would swarm through that hole and come at them. The monks closing the doors behind them would only stop them for a moment.

They appeared to be in a dining hall. Long, low tables ran the length of the room, with cushions placed at regular intervals for the monks to sit on. An open door and a serving window on the far wall led to the kitchen. Several round young faces with shaved heads peeked out.

Oh my God. The initiates.

Jana's mind raced. She only had a few seconds at most to come up with a plan, or they'd all be dead, these half-grown children with them.

What could they do? Think! Think!

Where could they hide? She tried to remember the layout of the monastery from the few minutes she'd had to look at it. A series of old wooden buildings clinging to the slope or perched on narrow ledges, exposed staircases connecting most of them.

Most of them. She had noticed, but not really thought of, the fact that she had seen several isolated buildings that did not seem to have stairs leading to them. She had assumed the stairs were out of sight, but were they?

"Tunnels!" she shouted as bullets hammered on the door. "Are there tunnels in the stone? If we can get in there, the drones won't have a signal. They can't follow!"

Tamang staggered up the her, clutching his wounded shoulder, his hand dripping with blood. He began to shout in Nepali.

One of the initiates, who looked about thirteen and wore robes that were too big for him, ran out of the kitchen shouting something.

"In there!" Tamang said.

His words were almost drowned out as another missile from the relentless fleet of drones blew the doors off their hinges, sending half a dozen monks flying.

Everyone rushed for the kitchen except for a few brave monks who charged the drones.

A few brave monks, plus Jacob.

To hell with this.

Dumping Bledshaw on the monk who had helped carry him, she rushed into the fray.

Tamang stayed behind, shouting to the monks and initiates, no doubt explaining again why they needed to get further inside the building.

And into a tunnel? Jana hadn't had time to confirm that.

If there was a tunnel, they might just have a chance.

If there wasn't, she'd rather go down fighting next to the man she loved.

But first, a weapon.

A spear lay next to one of the fallen monks. The sight of it brought back a teenage memory of a day with her father.

Bayonet practice.

"Chances are you'll never use a bayonet in your life," he had explained as her fourteen-year-old self stood holding a rifle fitted with a bayonet in front of a straw dummy. *"But it's a good workout and it helps build aggression."*

She had attacked that dummy with the ferocity of a lioness, her father never knowing that the aggression came from his frequent absences.

Jana decided to channel that angry young girl.

Planting her feet shoulder-width apart and turning her body slightly to the side, she let out a roar and charged.

She nailed a drone just as it swooped into the room. The point of the spear sparked off the metal sheath, and the drone shuddered and backed off. It swung around, training its machine gun on her. Jana thrust again, getting the spear shaft into the way of the rotors.

Her arms and shoulders jerked painfully as the rotors hit hard, and the drone spun upside down and landed in front of her.

The machine gun went off. A monk nearby leapt three feet into the air to avoid the bullets. Jana jabbed her spear into the exposed underbelly of the drone and sparks flew.

The machine gun stopped firing.

That didn't stop the other machines. More monks fell. One tackled a drone and, shielding his friends with his own body, fell to the floor as bullets churned his belly. Jacob destroyed the drone with his polearm.

A well-thrown dart took out the camera of the last drone, and as it fired blind a monk swung an ax and cleaved it in two.

A monk shouted something at them and gestured toward the kitchen. They all ran for it.

Through a steam-filled room with an open fireplace and a large pot full of bubbling soup. Then through a pantry and into a back hallway. Beyond was a doorway cut into the stone.

"Perfect!"

"Smart thinking," Jacob said, running beside her.

They entered a cool, cramped hallway passing into the mountainside. Behind they could hear the buzzing of the pursuing drones. Jana glanced back and just past a couple of stragglers she saw the first drone pass into the kitchen.

"Keep going!" she shouted, hoping Tamang would translate. "We have to get further in so the drones lose their signal!"

Tamang started saying something, but it got cut off by an explosion.

A drone had launched another missile. Luckily, the shot had been wide and hit the doorway into the stone passageway, the blast ripping through the pantry and taking out the drone itself.

Even so, shards of stone knocked down the last two monks. Their comrades grabbed them and carried them along.

The passageway began to turn and slope upwards. Torchlight glimmered further along, lighting their way. Jana glanced back through the dust cloud caused by the explosion. She didn't see any more drones, and her ears rang so badly from the detonation she wouldn't have heard them even if they were right on top of her.

She and the rest kept running.

Just as the pantry was disappearing around the bend, a drone passed through the cloud of dust and opened up with a machine gun.

The bullets ricocheted off the wall. A monk got grazed but otherwise no one got hit as they hurried around the bend and got out of sight.

Why had the last two drones missed? Was it because they were losing their signal already, and their operators couldn't maneuver or aim effectively?

Whatever the reason, Jana and her companions had bought themselves some time.

But only some time. Because the drone operators knew where they were.

If they had infantry coming as backup, she and the rest of the people in the monastery were screwed.

They might be screwed if they stayed here. If the drones could find the other end of this tunnel, they could launch missiles to blast both ends and seal them inside. Plus, most of the other monks were still exposed outside or in the vulnerable wooden buildings.

The abbot led them up the tunnel as it turned and ascended on a gentle slope. Their breath frosted the air, but Jana felt hot and a bit dizzy from the exertion. Her lungs heaved, punctuated by coughs from the dust billowing up from the last explosion.

A groan beside her made her look. Bledshaw, draped over the shoulder of a monk who carried him as if he weighed nothing more than a child, was coming to.

A few more steps and the tunnel opened out onto a storage room. Barrels and boxes filled much of the space. The wooden walls told her that they had entered another building, no doubt the one she had seen just above and to the right of the one where they had met the abbot. A door on the opposite wall was closed.

Jana moved over to it and listened. Through the ringing in her ears, she could hear distant gunfire and shouting, but no buzz of a drone nearby. Would she even be able to hear it with her ears ringing like that?

The abbot listened too, then looked at her and nodded.

He reached for the doorknob.

"Wait," Jana said, raising her hand to indicate her meaning. She turned to the assembled monks and initiates. "Does anyone here speak English?"

The smallest initiate in the crowd hurried up. He didn't look more than twelve.

"I English good! Best in school! I join monastery this year while remember English."

Jana looked around. No one else was volunteering. Jacob gave her a shrug.

Better than nothing, I suppose. Sure is better than my Nepali.

She bent over the little bald boy and slowly and clearly said, "Everyone needs to get into the tunnels."

She emphasized this by making a wide motion to encompass the crowd and then pointing to the tunnel.

The boy puzzled through this, then said, "They now."

"No, I mean everyone … " she pointed outside, " … in here." She pointed inside.

"They now. All now!"

A scream from outside.

"No. They aren't all inside. They need to—"

"They *know*!"

"What?"

The boy stared at her. His face lit up.

"Know!"

"What?"

"They know." He pointed to the tunnel.

"Are there more … " she pointed to the tunnel.

"Little. No, big! Many!"

The abbot placed a broad hand on his shoulder, and they spoke in Nepali for a moment. The initiate looked relieved to be speaking in his native language again.

The initiate turned back to Jana, thought for a moment, his lips moving silently, then said,

"He say us … " he pointed to himself, Jana, and the abbot " … go to temple. Them … " he pointed to everyone else. " … go … "

He stared off into space, mouth working, then gave a shrug. He motioned with his hands as if fighting.

"You want them to make a distraction while we go to the temple? Why?"

Blank stare.

Oops. Speaking too quickly.

"Why go to the temple?"

"I don't know say." He held up his fists, then splayed his fingers out. "We win."

"Winning sounds good," Jacob said.

"Sounds good to me too," Jana replied. She turned to the initiate. "Yes. They go fight. We go to the temple."

The initiate translated to the abbot. The old man looked her in the eye, and she saw a confidence there that buoyed her up.

She listened at the door again, then opened it a crack, prepared to run. She wouldn't put it past their attackers to have landed a drone on the other side to sit quietly waiting.

All she saw was an empty, candlelit hallway. The distant boom of an explosion told her they weren't safe.

The abbot peered over her shoulder, then stepped into the hallway. He still held the initiate by the shoulder and motioned for Jana to follow him to the left. He gestured for the others to go to the right from where the sounds of battle came.

As the group split up, Jana looked over her shoulder and caught Jacob's eye.

She hated seeing him go into danger, and she hated it even more when she couldn't be by his side.

CHAPTER NINETEEN

Jana followed the abbot as he and the initiate ran down a corridor past several closed doors. When they got to a larger front room with stone foundations and open windows looking out onto the mountains, her breath caught. Painted on the bare stone were religious images much like those found by the Canadian team in the medieval monastery.

She didn't have time to admire them, though, because out the window she saw several drones flying around, searching, hunting.

Hunting for the abbot.

Why target him? Was the information they sought to gain from him really that important? Whoever was looking for the *cyar mey* obviously thought he could stop them somehow, or give Jacob and Jana information that would stop them.

But what could a Buddhist monk in a rural area of Nepal know that could prove so crucial?

She hoped she'd live long enough to find out. The temple stood higher up the slope, isolated from and grander than all the other buildings.

It jutted out on a rocky crag, an ornate red pagoda roof held up by yellow pillars. It was open to the air, and inside Jana could make a giant status of a golden Buddha.

The temple was in such contrast to the Spartan buildings of the rest of the monastery she wondered if it had been built by someone else. Indeed, it did have a sense of age to it.

That question got shunted to the side as she looked at the only approach—a narrow set of stone steps that ran for a good hundred yards in plain view.

"There's no way we're getting up there alive," she said.

"What?" the initiate said.

She pointed to the stairs, then the drones circling around.

"No, no." The initiate pointed to a building adjoining their own on the other side of a small courtyard.

"There's a tunnel there?"

"What?"

She pointed back the way they came and made a gesture toward the ground.

"Yes!"

"OK … " she looked again at the courtyard. While it could have only been about ten yards wide, with those drones hovering nearby it seemed like miles.

But hesitation could kill them. While they were well away from the windows, sooner or later they'd get spotted, especially since there was no glass to reflect the light and obscure them.

They needed to run fast. Could she? Jana was barely keeping her breath in this rarified air. She still felt dizzy and her ears throbbed.

The abbot took a look at her, then closed his eyes, put his palms together, and took a long, deep breath. Jana tried to calm her racing heart and get enough oxygen into her lungs for the death run to come.

The abbot took a second deep breath, and a third …

… and then did something unexpected.

He opened his eyes, grabbed the initiate with one hand and Jana with the other, tucked them under his arms like a pair of oversized footballs, and sprinted across the room.

He leapt through the open window and out into the courtyard.

The drones responded immediately. From her jiggling, horizontal vantage point, Jana caught a glimpse of several of them swooping down.

A machine gun ripped the air, bullets cracking off the cobblestones all around them. The abbot leapt through another open window and into the building.

He didn't set them down, and he didn't stop. He sprinted down a hallway.

A moment later, an explosion blew them all forward.

The abbot staggered for a moment, righted himself, and kept on going.

He pelted down the hallway and around a corner. Through the ringing in Jana's ears, she could hear the buzz of pursuing drones. Still being carried like a delivery package, she couldn't see a thing.

The abbot got to a door, dumped Jana and the initiate on the floor, and opened it.

Just as Jana and the initiate rose, a drone came around the corner.

The abbot flung a knife at it, hitting the rotors and making it jerk crazily in the air.

That probably saved their lives because the bullets from its machine gun hit the wall across from them instead of tearing through them.

They rushed through the door and slammed it behind them before the killer drone righted itself.

Passing through a prayer room that was nothing more than a bare space with a statue of the Buddha in a niche in one wall, they opened another door into a larger room used for martial arts practice. Jana grabbed a spear. The abbot stocked up on some more shuriken and throwing knives, tucking them into various pockets of his robes that looked designed for the purpose. As he turned, Jana noticed blood on his back.

“He’s hurt!” she cried, pointing out the wound to the initiate.

There followed a quick conversation—concern on the initiate’s part, a quick dismissal by the abbot—and they ran across the room to the opposite door, passing through and closing it behind them.

Just in time. An explosion rocked the room they had just left. One of the missile drones had blasted its way in.

Maybe they’ll run out of missiles and they won’t be able to chase us through the buildings anymore.

Maybe the Easter Bunny will save you. You’re on your own with these two. Deal with it.

They hurried down a short passage past a couple of closed doors. At the end, the wooden walls gave way to stone. The entrance to the tunnel was arched, and above the arch was a delicately painted Buddha. Above it was painted a golden vajra.

They hurried into the torchlit tunnel, the path turning and rising upwards. Jana's lunge heaved. Her short break as luggage hadn't given her time to fully catch her breath.

By the time they made it to the top, she was gasping and staggering.

The sight that met her was a surprise. They hadn’t come out beside or in front of the Buddha, but behind it. The giant Buddha, decorated in gleaming gold leaf, had its back to them and blocked the view of the scene outside. Heady incense sweetened the sharp mountain air.

For a moment, the three of them stopped and listened. They could hear drones in the distance, but nothing close.

The abbot led them slowly around the statue. Jana noticed the bloodstain on his back had spread, but if the old man noticed, he didn’t let it affect him. Keeping to the shadows, he crouched low and peeked around the base of the statue, ducking back a second later.

He led them back to the doorway and whispered something to the initiate, who turned to Jana.

“Bad thing there.”

“A drone. One of the flying things?” She imitated a drone with her hand flying through the air.

“Yes.”

It must have landed and is facing the statue.

“How many?” Jana asked.

“What?”

"One? Two? Three?" Jana held up her fingers as she counted.

“Two.” The boy held up two fingers.

The abbot said something and gently pushed the initiate back into the tunnel. The boy looked reluctant to go but did as he was told. Then the old man turned and pointed to himself and Jana.

“You go fight bad things,” the initiate said. “He go vajra. Bad things go.”

Jana didn’t know what he meant by that but wasn’t going to question it. They didn’t have time for long explanations in broken English. The abbot seemed to know what he was doing, and with that bloodstain still spreading, it didn’t look like he had much time to do it.

They crept back to the corner of the giant statue, Jana with her spear at the ready and the abbot with a pair of shuriken, one in each hand.

The abbot said a short, sharp word Jana took for “now” and she leapt out into view, the abbot right beside her.

In front of the statue was a large area for worship with a few smoking braziers of incense. The temple was a simple flat floor with no wall at the edge, only a row of yellow columns holding up the roof. Sitting at the far edge of the floor were a pair of drones with machine guns, one facing the statue and one facing outwards, no doubt with its camera trained on the staircase.

The abbot flung a shuriken and hit the one facing them straight in the camera, shattering it. He followed with the second shuriken, which clanged off the thin metal plating.

Jana charged, angling a bit to the right to avoid the blinded drone’s line of fire. To her surprise, it didn’t open up on them. As she ran, the drone facing away from them started its rotors. She had to get there before it turned and spotted her.

Sprinting across the polished floor, she saw to her terror the drone lift up out of reach and turn. She changed the grip on her spear and threw it, aiming for the vulnerable rotors.

It hit the metal sheath, slid up across it, and the tip of her spear got in the path of the rotors.

The spear flew away, along with a portion of the rotor, and the drone fell on its side, the rotors smacking into the wooden floor. The drone spun out and plummeted off the edge of the temple floor to roll down the cliff.

The abbot rushed up beside the other drone and gave it a hard kick that broke the metal sheath and shattered the electronics within.

Jana looked out over the monastery buildings scattered on the slope below and the vast space of the valley beyond.

At least a dozen drones were converging on their position and aiming for the temple.

No way could they fight them off.

"We need to … "

She turned and saw the abbot running away.

Uh-oh.

She was about to run too when she saw what he was running to.

The immense golden Buddha sat on a plinth in the lotus position. In his hands rested a giant vajra.

Jana stared. It was of gleaming brass and looked to be about a third the size of the Royal Vajra.

Maybe that's why the drone didn't fire blind.

The abbot ran right up to the vajra, closed his eyes, and placed his hands on either end of it, having to stretch out his arms to do so.

Jana glanced over her shoulder. The drones were approaching. When she looked back, she saw the abbot still standing there, oblivious to the danger and the bloodstain that had spread across his back to run down his pants.

The initiate peeked around the corner of the plinth.

"Get back! Get back!" Jana shouted, running toward him.

The boy didn't move, but instead stared openmouthed out at the approaching drones as if frozen.

The buzz of their approach grew louder, but began to get drowned out by another noise, a low hum that steadily rose in volume.

Jana looked behind her again. The drones were in range. They'd open fire any moment.

CHAPTER TWENTY

Jana gestured desperately at the young initiate peeking around the corner. The approaching drones would see him for sure, and she knew their operators would show him no mercy.

Then a light to her right distracted her. That hum she had heard grew louder, and she stared at the oversized brass vajra held between the Buddha's hands.

It had begun to pulse and glow with a pure golden light. The abbot still stood before it, his hands on either end just next to the gilded hands of the statue.

The hum increased in volume, and Jana felt it reverberating through her body like she was standing in front of a speaker at a rock concert. The vajra pulsed, the glow waxing until it was difficult to look at directly. The abbot became nothing but a silhouette.

Despite her curiosity, Jana could not stay distracted from the looming sense of death for long. She whirled around to look back out across the valley.

The drones were closing in. At any moment, they'd fire. Several had missiles, enough to blow this whole temple apart.

There was nowhere to run.

Then—a pulse of sound and light that forced Jana to her knees and made her cover her eyes with her hands.

That lasted only a moment, followed by silence.

Blinking through the afterimages, she saw something that made her gasp with wonder.

All the drones were falling out of the sky.

Jana struggled to her feet. With a glance at the initiate, who looked as shocked as she did, she nervously walked over to the edge of the temple floor.

Below was the steep rocky slope to which the other monastery buildings clung. The slope was scattered with fallen drones. Some had landed on the roofs of various monastery buildings.

All of them were inert, their electronics giving off smoke.

An electromagnetic pulse. That's the only thing that could have done this.

She turned to the abbot, who stood erect, stepping down from the plinth. He turned to the Buddha, bowed deeply, then went over to the incense holder and lit some joss sticks. The initiate scampered out from behind the statue and stood beside him, facing the statue with his palms pressed together in front of his heart.

Stunned, Jana looked at the smoking ruins of the drone fleet and back at the Buddhist abbot and his initiate. The vajra rested inert between the hands of the Buddha as if nothing had happened.

Jana wanted to question them, but knew the initiate didn't have sufficient English to explain what just happened. He might not have sufficient Nepali. What had just occurred might be beyond words.

Down the slope, monks began to peek out of windows and doorways. After a moment, they rushed out to help the wounded and check on the dead. Jana spotted Jacob, Tamang, and Bledshaw come out of a nearby building.

She waved. They spotted her and started to climb the steps up to the temple, looking over their shoulders, on the watch for more drones.

But there were no more drones. From her vantage point, Jana could see for miles. The skies were clear.

Jana waited in silence as her companions climbed the stairs toward her. She felt strange, as if she had stepped into some surreal parallel world. The rational part of her mind explained that the vajra was part of some large electromagnetic system stored inside the Buddha. While that made logical sense, it left way more questions than it answered.

Like why a powerful electromagnetic pulse generator was hidden inside a Buddha in a monastery in the middle of nowhere.

Or how it worked when there wasn't any electric power grid within fifty miles.

Or how the Royal Vajra and others depicted in early art could have functioned centuries before the invention of electricity.

Or … or … or …

Jana's head trying to rationalize away all the reasons that her logical explanation was obviously the *wrong* explanation.

For once, logic just didn't make sense.

The three men made it to the top.

"What happened?" Jacob asked between deep gulps of air.

"I don't know," Jana admitted. "The vajra in that statue's hands glowed and hummed and burnt out the drones. I think it was an electromagnetic pulse."

Jacob cocked his head. "How?"

“I don’t know. The abbot did it somehow.”

Tamang and Bledshaw sat down heavily on the edge of the floor, their legs dangling over the side.

“You two all right?”

Bradshaw shook his head. "I got knocked out cold by that explosion. I'm not cut, and nothing's broken. I'm still pretty shaken, but I’ll be all right in a bit.”

She looked at Tamang. Someone had wrapped a bandage around his arm, but the cloth was already soaked with blood.

“The bullet went clean through the muscle,” he told her. "I've lost some blood, but I'll be fine."

Jana thought that assessment overly optimistic. They needed to get both men down to the military base in the next valley over for treatment.

Actually, after all this firing, she figured the Nepalese armed forces would be speeding their way here.

Assuming they hadn't been affected by the electromagnetic pulse, too. Just how powerful had it been?

She turned to the abbot, who was just finishing up his prayers with the initiate. The two monks walked over to them.

“Vajra save us,” the initiate said in English.

Jana smiled and put a hand on his shoulder. “Yes, it did. Tamang, could you translate while I speak to the abbot?”

“All right.”

“Ask him how his wound is.”

There was a brief interchange, Tamang sounding incredulous.

“He says he isn’t wounded.”

“There’s a rip in his robes and a bloodstain over his entire back.”

Another brief interchange.

“He says he’s no longer wounded.”

Jana got a weird tingly feeling. She looked at the abbot, who treated her to a serene smile.

“Could you ask him what just happened?” she whispered.

Tamang asked, then asked something else about the answer. Then followed a long exchange with Tamang, obviously not getting whatever it was the abbot was trying to explain to him. Jana had the feeling that she wouldn't get it either.

Tamang turned to her. “Briefly put, he says he used the energy of the earth to overload the electronics in the drones. The vajra channels this energy.”

"This is what we'd been talking about before. But how?"

"He says it's spiritual."

"Come on. There's got to be a mechanism."

Tamang stared at the Buddha, clutching in injured arm.

"I'm not so sure about that," he whispered.

Jacob pulled out his phone and looked at it. "My phone is dead."

Bledshaw and Tamang followed suit. Their phones were dead too. The abbot said something, and Tamang translated.

"He says every piece of electronic equipment in the valley is destroyed. He apologizes for our phones."

"The abbot saved our lives," Bradshaw said. "He hardly needs to apologize."

Tamang cut in. "He says we need to go down and help the wounded. We'll talk more later. He has some things to tell you about that picture you have of the archaeological site."

***

The late afternoon sun had dipped behind the mountains, leaving the valley in chill shadow. Jana and her companions had suffered a long, exhausting afternoon collecting the dead and tending to the wounded. Luckily both Jacob and Bledshaw had first aid kits in their packs, and a couple of the monks this monastery of warriors were versed in treating wounds.

Still, the losses had been heavy. About a quarter of the monks were dead or injured. If it hadn't been for the vajra, Jana had no doubt that virtually all of them would have been killed.

The army had shown up in force within a couple of hours. The abbot himself had gone down to the monastery entrance and spoke with the commanding officer. Their minder, Corporal Koirala, also spoke with them along with Tamang and the local mayor. When it was all done, the troops went down to the bottom of the slope and took up positions, pointing a row of heavy machine guns toward the sky backed up with some Stinger antiaircraft missiles.

"What did they say?" Jana asked Tamang. "I'm amazed they didn't ask more questions or cross-examine the foreigners in the group."

"The monks here have a lot of local respect." The Nepalese-American glanced up at the golden Buddha. "I can see why."

"Do they have any idea who did this?"

"Their commander is convinced it's the Chinese. The rebels don't have the capability and there's no other force nearby except the Indians and he doesn't think it's them. While the Indians want to muscle in on the territory here, they wouldn't want to jeopardize their relations with other south Asian countries and the West. They're content to sit back and wait for China to be the bad guys."

They had examined the drones and found no markings except for the serial numbers on the parts. Jana supposed those could be traced, but they didn't have the time right now and besides, all their phones were dead. The soldiers had taken a couple of the drones to examine them.

Jacob had tried his satellite phone and it was dead too. They were temporarily cut off from the outside world unless they wanted to use Nepalese army equipment.

"So what's the army's plan?" Jana asked.

"They've radioed back to the capital to get reinforcements and further orders."

"At least their equipment wasn't affected."

"The electromagnetic pulse, if that's what it was, didn't reach beyond this valley."

"What do they want us to do?"

"They didn't say. I got the impression that they weren't quite sure what to do about us."

"They don't think we had anything to do with it, do they?"

It wouldn't be the first time CIA agents got blamed for someone else's misdeeds.

"Not directly. But they see us as a bunch of big targets endangering everything around us."

Jana sighed. "Well, I can't argue with that."

Jacob stepped up. "I think the real question we need to ask is, if Dr. Harlow is behind this, why would he want to create tensions between China and Nepal? We're on the brink of war here."

"And if war comes, the Indian army is going to roll right into here, and there's nothing the Nepalese can do about it," Tamang said.

"It could be the start of World War Three," Bledshaw said. "Both China and India are nuclear powers."

"I don't see how this helps Dr. Harlow. If he already has the Royal Vajra, why cause trouble? And if he's looking for something else in this region, a pair of massing armies is the last thing he'd want."

"Unless it's someone else," Jana said.

“All right, but who?” Tamang asked.

Jana and Jacob traded a look. They didn’t have to answer that, at least for themselves.

They knew the answer—The Order.

The Order was a shadowy organization that Jana’s father Aaron had been fighting for years. While their motives remained unclear, the methods were ruthless and their capabilities vast. They had been behind numerous attacks, trying to destabilize various global hotspots, and may have supplied and manipulated the Islamist group The Sword of the Righteous into attempting to set off a nuclear device in Rome.

They had been assuming Dr. Harlow was behind this because he was searching for relics of this so-called Civilization X, but what if it had been The Order? Or what if one was manipulating the other? What if they were one and the same?

Jana’s head spun with the possibilities, and she knew Jacob Snow well enough to know that he was thinking along the same lines.

It was good they were thinking the same thing because they couldn't speak their minds. The Order had infiltrated the CIA to the point that they could trust no one, not even a seemingly good man like Agent Arjun Tamang.

Jana felt like she was betraying a brave and loyal colleague. Still, she had no choice. Security had to take first place in front of personal loyalty.

God, what a dirty world we live in.

While that had once made her hate her father’s work, now she appreciated it. It was dirty, yes, but vital.

“So what’s our next move?” Bledshaw asked.

For a moment, no one answered. They were still trying to think of a good course of action when the little initiate came up to them and bowed.

"Abbot, see you now.”

Jana smiled at the boy. "Thank you."

I sure hope the abbot has some ideas because I have no clue what we should do next.

CHAPTER TWENTY ONE

Jacob sat cross-legged on a mat in a Spartan room devoid of any other furnishings and lit by a single oil lamp. Jana, Bledshaw, and Tamang sat beside him. That little initiate who had acted as translator for Jana served them tea and a simple meal of rice and steamed vegetables.

Before them, sitting on the mat at the same level as they did, was the abbot.

The initiate finished serving, bowed, and left. They ate in silence for a time, the abbot studying them as he slowly brought his chopsticks to his mouth.

At last, they finished their meal, and the abbot addressed them. Tamang translated.

"I have been meditating on the theft of the Royal Vajra and the spate of recent attacks, not the least of which was the attack on our very own Order of the Sacred Lotus. I believe I know who might be behind these attacks."

Everyone shifted in their seats. Jacob leaned forward, listening to every word from Tamang's mouth but focusing only on the abbot.

"There was a wise monk who lived in this monastery more than two hundred years ago. He would isolate himself in one of the caves high up in the mountain peaks for months at a time, and when he did this, he would have visions. Many of these visions have come true. Others have not, and are considered prophecies for the future. One of his prophecies might pertain to what we have faced today.

"The monk prophesized that the great spiritual land of Tibet would be taken over by a godless empire that forbade spirituality. Not content with oppressing their own people, they wanted to destroy the spirituality of all other nations, and started with Tibet. Other great powers hated this empire but feared its strength and decided to placate and trade with them rather than fight the just fight."

Jacob and Jana traded a look. He had an idea where this was going.

The abbot went on.

"The monk predicted that after the empire had taken over Tibet and oppressed its people, it would be content for a time, ringed by other great powers and not daring to expand its boundaries. But a monk of great martial prowess would grow discontent with this status quo and wish to break it. Only thus would the monks and nuns of Tibet be free to practice their spiritual path. He will devise a plan to tap in to the power of the *cyar mey* and use it to unleash devastation on the godless empire. The empire, thinking it was under attack by one of its neighbors, would start a war that it would eventually lose, thus freeing Tibet. The prophecy said that many millions would die in this war, but that the monk would think it was all for the good because the only thing that mattered to him was to free Tibet."

Silence fell in the little room. Jacob licked his lips and spoke.

"Did the … um … prophecy say who this monk would be?"

"No. But I can think of only one other monastery in the Himalayas besides this one that practices the great martial arts. It is the monastery of the Order of the Invisible Lotus, about a hundred miles from here, not far from the Chinese border. We do not have any contact with them and have not for more than a hundred years. While we practice our martial arts in order to progress further on the path of enlightenment, they use it only for violence. A hundred years ago, when control over the hinterland was weak, they oppressed the peasants, forcing them to work harder and harder and taking most of their produce. The Order of the Invisible Lotus no longer wanted to live off voluntary donations, but instead taxed the peasants terribly, as did many other monasteries in Tibet. It is a shame, but it is true. Many monasteries crushed the peasants underfoot, and that gave the Chinese Communists an excuse to invade. They claimed they were freeing the peasants, although the peasants only ended up under a different master.

"While this oppression was common in Tibet, it was not so in Nepal and the peasants rebelled. The Order of the Invisible Lotus crushed them brutally, destroying them in a series of lopsided battles the peasants could not hope to win. They did not kill any man who they did not have to in battle, because they needed them to tend the fields, but instead took out their wrath on those who could do less work—the elderly and many women. The king, weak as he was in the valley of Kathmandu, could only protest. All the right-guided monastic orders cut their ties with the Order of the Invisible Lotus."

Silence for a moment. Jacob plucked up the courage to speak.

"And you think that this rogue order is behind all this?"

The abbot nodded. "They do not have a vajra, and have always pressured us to give up ours. We would not do that, for it is the sacred heart of our order, and it became unthinkable after what they did to their own people."

"So you think they stole the Royal Vajra?"

"Perhaps, and they tried to kill me, so I couldn't tell you about them. It is the only other one. You see, that photo you found that the archaeologist took, it was an illustration of the vajra's power, and just enough of the text around it was visible for me to recognize it from an ancient text, the one that contains the prophecy."

"But how would a martial order of monks have gunmen to break into the museum? How would they have a fleet of drones?"

"We have isolated ourselves from technology here in order to avoid distractions on our path to enlightenment. That does not mean we are entirely against technology. Some of the more severely injured monks have been sent to the military hospital the armed forces in the valley set up, for example. On occasion we use a telephone in a nearby city in order to have quick communication with other orders. Thus, the Order of the Invisible Lotus would be under no constraints to avoid modern technology. Indeed, they may have embraced it."

"But why do all this?"

"Because the prophecy says the man who will start the war will be a monk of great martial prowess. None in our own order would do this, so it must be them."

"Couldn't it be someone else?" Jacob asked, unconvinced.

"No one else knows about the true power of the Royal Vajra, not even the royal family itself. If they had, they would have never let the Royal Vajra leave the palace. Like so many, they have forgotten their heritage, begun to believe that the truths of their ancestors are nothing but myths and exaggerations."

Tamang looked at the floor as he translated this.

Bledshaw cut in. "How well do these monks know the mountains? You said they're a hundred miles from here. Could they have made it here undetected?"

The army was already scouring the foothills, and in the distance, they had seen helicopters circling around the lower portions of the mountains. As far as Jacob and his friends knew, they had found nothing.

"Oh, yes. The Order of the Invisible Lotus are masters of the mountains. Many are from Sherpa stock, and unlike us, who remain mostly in the monastery in order to pray and live a pure life, they often go out into the wilderness to harden their bodies and explore. I have no doubt that they know many secret passes and caves so they can travel undetected."

Jacob nodded. That made sense, although he still had a hard time believing that some monastic order in the Himalayas would have sourced an entire drone fleet and a large crew of skilled operators. The monks might have been the foot soldiers, but he still felt Dr. Harlow or The Order was behind it.

"We should check out this monastery," Bledshaw said.

"How are we going to get inside?" Tamang asked.

Jacob looked him up and down. "I don't think you're fit enough to continue the mission."

The CIA agent gave him a steady gaze. "I'm here for the whole thing. Besides, you need a translator."

"You sure?"

"Don't worry. I won't slow you down. But back to my question. How do we get inside?"

"Can't we just ask the authorities to search the place?"

Tamang shook his head. "I already know their answer. They won't believe a Buddhist monastery would do this, and the repercussions of searching a monastery could be problematic for the government."

"They nearly slaughtered an entire monastery with us in it!"

"You think I don't know that?" Tamang said, gesturing to his bandaged arm. "But all we have to go on is a prophecy from a rival monastery, and while I believe the abbot is telling us the truth, there's no way the authorities are going to buy it."

"You believe in this prophecy?" Jacob asked, surprised. Tamang was a pretty secular guy.

"I believe that Vajra dropped the entire drone fleet and miraculously healed his wound. And I believe a far bigger vajra is missing."

Jacob didn't have an answer to that.

"It does go with what we know about the Order of the Invisible Lotus," Bledshaw said.

Jacob did a double take. "Wait. What?"

"Our initial assessment is that the most likely candidate for the theft of the Royal Vajra is this monastic order, perhaps with the backing of Dr. Harlow."

"And you didn't think to share this with the rest of us?" Jana said with a frown.

"Why were you holding out on us?" Jacob said.

Tamang looked confused.

Bledshaw gave a little shrug. “We weren’t failing to share intelligence. We were simply not sharing a theory.”

“Wonderful,” Jana groaned. She looked like she wanted to smack him. Jacob wanted to smack him too.

“We?” Tamang asked. “Who’s we?”

"That's classified," Bradshaw said.

Tamang didn’t look happy with that answer, but his training had accustomed him to being left in the dark about certain aspects of the missions he’d been on. It was something Jacob had to deal with too. He never liked it, but it was part of the game.

He never liked it when those obfuscations turned out to be direct lies.

Keep your eye on Bledshaw, he reminded himself.

The abbot said something, and there was a brief conversation between him and Tamang before the rest of them got a translation.

“He wants to know if we’re going to scout out the monastery.”

“I don’t think we have much choice,” Jacob said. “It’s our only lead at this point.”

The others nodded. The abbot picked up a little bell next to his tray and rang it. The initiate entered, carrying a rolled-up map that he gave to his master.

The abbot unrolled it, and they saw it was a detailed topo of a mountainous region with a few villages scattered in the valleys. He began to point out key features and explain.

"The monastery is like ours, built into the slope of a mountain overlooking a valley. The village below is bigger than the one here, and over in the next valley is a mid-sized town with a paved road running to it. Don't let that fool you. It is still very remote. The monastery itself paid for the road to be paved a year ago, and we find that suspicious. Perhaps they wanted to run vehicles with heavier loads along it, although we don't know what for. That road is their weakness. There is no way you can approach the monastery without being spotted. The main stairs and all the back passes—here, here, and here—are closely guarded. You would never pass the sentries unseen, no matter how good your training. But you could come unseen on the back of a truck right into the town and then by a smaller vehicle into the village. We have local contacts who can help you. From there, it is up to you.”

Jacob studied the map. He saw a few higher peaks fringing the valley, much like the one they were in. He pointed at one.

"Could your contact get us somewhere up there? It looks like it gives a clear view of the monastery. With a good telescope we could see all the movement within the monastery grounds."

"Yes, we could get you there, but they might be watching that spot. I am sure they will have numerous sentries spread out in a wide area."

"It's a risk we'll have to take," Jacob said. "We need more intel before going in, assuming we do go in."

"I think you'll find the Order of the Invisible Lotus is the guilty party," the abbot insisted. "They are the only ones who would take the prophecy seriously."

Them and a whole bunch of other people, Jacob thought. *You're a bit too isolated here, my friend.*

I envy you.

CHAPTER TWENTY TWO

It had been a long, grueling 24 hours, but now Jacob could finally settle behind a compact and powerful telescope and take a look at the monastery of the Order of the Invisible Lotus.

Tamang had arranged a ride on a military helicopter back to Kathmandu, where they had geared up. Tamang had received further medical care, and they hopped on another helicopter to get to a town closer to the region where they needed to go. The abbot's contact met them there. He was a truck driver who made his living delivering goods to remote towns. On the side he delivered messages for the monks. From there they endured a long, bumpy ride in the back of a truck before having to hide beneath piles of imported clothing as the came into town.

The contact parked inside a garage and after a quick meal guided them out of town and into the mountains under the cover of darkness.

The ascent had been terrifying. While Jacob had at last acclimatized to the altitude, the night was frigid, the wind biting, and there was no path, only a scramble up rocks and the occasional traverse across nearly sheer cliffs. They took the easiest route and none of it required ropes, but doing it in the dark sure didn't help.

Tamang, with his arm in a sling, had done it all one-handed, joking all the way that if he had been a true Nepalese, he could have done it with no hands. The fact that he could do it at all was miracle enough for Jacob.

Now they had settled into a shallow bowl barely big enough to accommodate them as the sun peeked over the mountains to the east. To their west, past a lower ridge of jagged peaks, lay the valley owned by the Order of the Invisible Lotus. On the far side of that valley was the monastery. It glowed golden in the rising sun. Jacob scanned the area with his telescope.

Like the abbot had said, it was arranged in a similar way to his own monastery. Buildings were on various levels of the slope, looking as if they were growing out of the rock. In fact, they were made not of wood but of the same stone, adding to the impression. Jacob suspected this place had tunnels too.

And those stone buildings looked pretty defensible. There were arrow slits, a product of an earlier time that could just as easily be used for guns, plus there was a high wall around the whole thing. Monks made the rounds on the catwalk, keeping watch.

Even with the telescope's good magnification, Jacob had trouble figuring out which buildings were which. He suspected that was on purpose. Smoke coming out of one of the central buildings hinted at a kitchen and mess, and the building at the summit with the double doors may very well be the temple, but he couldn't be sure. Just down the slope from that building was one where he could see a shortwave radio antenna, an incongruent sight in a medieval monastery.

He got more intel from the space between the buildings. Distant figures moved about, bald men dressed in black robes. Once he spotted a pair carrying a large, modern steel crate between them, just the right proportions to hold an attack drone.

Jacob kept studying the monastery, patient and calm. Tamang was with him while Bledshaw and Jana kept guard at the two easiest approaches to their position. They were miles from the nearest habitation and above the line of vegetation, so they didn't have to worry about locals. But the abbot had warned them the monks would be on the lookout.

Jacob had been watching since sunrise three hours ago, and he would continue to keep watching until he saw something worth seeing. He wasn't going to barge into that place without some solid intel that they were involved.

On the fourth hour of his vigil, he got it.

Two men emerged from one of the buildings lower down the slope, the same building the monks carrying the crate had entered. But these two men were dressed in western fashions. As they came out of the shadow of the building and into the light, he saw they had hair, and not only that, one of them had blond hair.

"Tamang, check this out."

The Nepalese-American sidled on up to the eyepiece.

"Well, look at that, this whole mountain range is filled with white boys!"

"I bet they're not there for martial arts training."

"Nope. Probably drone training, and they're the trainers. The abbot told me this monastery is closed off to all visitors, so this makes a couple of Anglos hanging around doubly suspicious."

Jacob took over at the eyepiece again and saw the pair stop between the buildings and talk with a monk. It was far too distant to try and read lips. Even with the telescope, the figures were tiny.

The monk led the two Anglos up the stairs past several buildings before they entered the topmost one, the building Jacob assumed to be the temple.

"Hey, Tamang, I think—"

His words got cut off by a pistol shot right behind him.

Jacob spun around in time to see a black-robed monk topple back off the edge of the natural bowl in which they hid. A second one leaped in and kicked the pistol out of Tamang's hand.

Having no time to grab his MP5, Jacob swung at the monk, only to end up upside down and flying toward the edge of the bowl. He only just managed to grab the lip of the bowl and stop himself tumbling down a slope to bash his head on countless jagged rocks.

He hauled himself up and saw the monk knock Tamang unconscious with a single blow. Then he spun around and faced Jacob.

Jacob got in a fighting stance and assessed his opponent. He could take on your average soldier easily. Even your average Green Beret was no big deal.

He had a feeling this guy was not going to be so easy.

A spinning kick nearly took Jacob's head off, and ducking it left him open for the follow-up sweep to the legs that laid him flat. Jacob only just managed to roll out of the way of a foot that would have caved his face in, then had to roll further to avoid another kick.

He bumped against the side of the depression and had nowhere left to go.

The monk swung down …

… then jerked as a shot burst through his chest.

He gasped, staggered, and fell.

Bledshaw stood behind him with an AR-15 in his grip.

"Thanks," Jacob gasped, getting up and grabbing his own weapon.

Jana appeared as well, and they all looked around. They didn't see any more monks in sight.

"Slipped right by us," Bledshaw said. "They must have been mountain goats to get here any other way than the ones we were guarding."

Jacob checked on Tamang. "Out cold. Saved my life, though. We need to recon the area. There might be more. We don't want them warning the monastery."

"No need to worry about that," a familiar voice called.

Jana's face lit up. "Dad?"

"The one and only."

Aaron Peters came into view, clambering up the steep mountainside.

"Where the hell did you come from?" Jacob asked. "I thought you were on R and R."

"That's what they told me about you too. I came out because this is big, really big. Of more immediate concern is this patrol. There were three of them. Two came for you, and one stayed behind to warn the monastery via radio. He didn't get the chance."

"Thanks, but what are you doing here?"

Aaron looked at Bledshaw. "Same reason he is. I think Dr. Harlow is behind this, but he's got help now. Major help."

Jacob and Jana exchanged a glance. The Order was in on this too?

Great. Just when I thought things couldn't get harder.

"Help? From who?" the assistant director of the Antiquities Division asked.

"Just another powerful group that wants to wreck everything good in the world. That's all you need to know." He turned to Tamang. "Who's the stiff?"

"Arjun Tamang. CIA agent. He's not a stiff, just unconscious. Saved my life. That was the initial shot you heard."

"The next shot was by myself, which also saved your life," Bledshaw said. "So care to enlighten me as to who this gentleman is and who's helping Dr. Harlow?"

"None of your business," Jacob and Jana said in unison. They looked at each other and laughed.

"I cannot—"

"You can and you will," Jacob snapped. "Don't like being left in the dark? Then don't do it to other people like you do constantly. So Aaron, what else do you know about this monastery?"

"The intel is vague but there's at least a dozen outsiders sheltering there. Most are drone operators who have been training the monks. Luckily, they don't have too many drones left. You guys took most of them out."

Jacob moved back to the telescope and checked out the monastery. The monks moved about as normal. He had worried that the thin mountain air would carry the sound of the shots to them. Then he realized the wind was blowing away from the monastery and toward them. That probably kept them from hearing.

"Why didn't you tell us you were coming?" Jana asked.

Her father shrugged. "Didn't have time. You guys were moving fast, as always, plus I didn't want to go to the American embassy. It's being watched by the Chinese and who knows who else."

"Are the Chinese involved in this?" Bledshaw asked.

"Not that we can tell."

"What about the Indians?"

"No. Enough for now. You're not going to play a game of twenty questions and figure out who it is we're not telling you about. Suffice it to say that I don't trust you enough."

Bledshaw and Aaron glared at each other for a moment. Jacob was impressed. Not many people could meet Aaron Peters' gaze and hold it.

"You're being foolish," Bradshaw said. "But we don't have time to argue. Sooner or later that patrol will need to check in and when they don't, another patrol will come looking for them. We need to hide the bodies and shift position."

"Agreed," Aaron said. "We'll take the radio and our Nepalese friend can listen in once he wakes up. I have a camp with a view of the monastery. We can head there once we clean up."

"And then what?" Bledshaw asked. "We have to get into that monastery and collect intel. I don't suppose you have a plan for getting into the monastery?"

Aaron Peters smiled. "As a matter of fact, I do."

CHAPTER TWENTY THREE

Jana's relief at her father joining them was tinged with worry. He was supposed to be resting back in the States. He'd been in the field for years and needed time to adjust to ordinary life again. And yet here he was on yet another mission, a mission in a region unfamiliar to him.

Like Jacob, and like herself, he didn't speak any of the local languages and he wasn't familiar with the geopolitics or local situation.

At least Tamang had woken up quickly enough. They had cleaned the scene, dumped the bodies down a narrow ravine, and moved to Aaron's camp, where he had been monitoring the monastery. It was on the same jagged ridge not far from their own spot. It was the best vantage point, which is why he had picked it just like they had.

That's how he had spotted them, and also spotted the patrol creeping up on them.

The rest of the day had been spent in rest and planning. Tamang had followed the radio chatter as the base station in the monastery asked several times for the patrol to respond. At last, they sent out extra patrols to look for them.

By evening, they had. While Jana and the rest had hidden the bodies, these monks knew the terrain all too well. Now, the entire monastery was on alert.

What worried her most was a numerical code that had been sent over the air just as the sun was setting. All the patrols radioed back, confirming receipt.

The airwaves went silent after that.

Now, Jana and her team were moving through a frigid and snowbound pass on the back side of the slope the monastery stood on. Her father's recon, aided by some called-in satellite imagery from his satellite phone, had located a little-used pass that got them close to the monastery. From there, they'd try to sneak in. If that didn't work, they'd blast their way in. Aaron had brought a couple of rocket-propelled grenade launchers. The MGK Bur (Malogabaritnyy Granatomotnyy Kompleks "Bur" or Compact Grenade-launching System "Auger") was a high-explosive antipersonnel weapon, firing a thermobaric charge equal to six kilos of TNT. The RMG (*Reaktivnaya*

Mnogotselevaya Granata, or "rocket-propelled multi-purpose grenade") was a bunker buster, good for blasting holes in stone walls and taking out whatever was on the other side.

It was crazy that an archaeology professor knew all this. Jana supposed she was the only one who did, unless there were other archaeology Ph.D.s out there who had a top-level CIA operative for a father.

Both grenade launchers were Russian, which made for an extra bit of obfuscation.

Confuse the enemy when at all possible, her father always told her.

They trudged along the narrow defile, the Himalayan wind howling up it to buffet their backs. What should have given them a helpful push was more hinderance than help. It made them stumble on the icy stones and froze them to their bones despite their mountain gear.

The only one who didn't seem affect by it was Tamang, who gamely strode along, one arm still in a sling, a big bruise on his face clearly visible even in the dim starlight, and an earpiece in his ear to listen to the chatter on the radio strapped to his pack.

There was nothing to listen to. Since that code was transmitted hours before, the airwaves had remained dead.

Despite her chill and her fatigue, Jana kept alert, eyes scanning the shadows for enemies. Her father was scouting somewhere up ahead, but even his presence couldn't entirely reassure her. There had to be guards somewhere along this path.

And then they found one, a dark form lying in a patch of snow. Jana peered at the monk and saw his neck was twisted in an unnatural angle.

Not far beyond, the trail humped over a cut on the edge of a higher ridge. A low whistle from a shadow told them where her father was.

He emerged from the dark as if made from it. They huddled around.

"All right," he whispered at a level that barely carried over the howling of the wind. "Just over that hump, we'll get to the upper corner of the wall surrounding the monastery grounds. It's ten feet tall. I've already put a rope ladder to the top. The sentry on duty has been neutralized."

The sentry has been neutralized. You mean you killed the sentry.

Something squirmed inside her. While she had plenty of enemy blood on her hands, she didn't like seeing this side to her father, no matter how necessary it was.

"What about the other sentries?" Bledshaw asked.

"Not very many, as far as I can tell. None close. But we got to hurry." He turned to Tamang. "You guard the ladder."

"I can get up one-handed."

"I'm sure you can, but we need someone guarding our rear."

Tamang's posture told her he wasn't happy with this. It did make sense, though.

"All right," he said, the reluctance clear in his voice despite being barely audible.

Her father put a hand on his shoulder. "We'll fetch you if we need a translator."

Jana felt they might need a translator along with them, not on call, but who else to leave in the rearguard? Jacob was too valuable a fighter, and no one trusted Bledshaw.

It took her a second to realize someone else could have kept the rearguard—herself. Did her dad not want to leave her alone? Or did he think she couldn't be relied upon not to sneak after them to get into the action?

Without another word, Aaron led them over the lower ridgetop, the higher ridge blotting the stars to their right, the valley below suddenly coming into view. The distant lights of the village looked warm and welcoming.

Not for her. She wouldn't enjoy a peaceful hearth for a while, if ever.

Because if these guys were as good fighters as the monks of their rival monastery, she was in for a long night, or perhaps a brutally short one.

They got to the wall, an old stone edifice with enough cracks that an expert climber like her dad could get up, and came to the rope ladder. It was made of black rope that made it all but invisible in the night, outlined by the dimmest of reflections of starlight off the stone.

Aaron went first, followed by Jacob, then herself, then Bledshaw. Tamang disappeared into a shadow to keep watch.

As Jana got onto the catwalk, she crouched low against the parapet, trying to make herself as small of a target as possible. The monastery buildings were dark and quiet shapes in the night. Nearby stood the largest building, the one Jacob took to be a temple.

She scanned the wall, looking for other guards.

The only one she saw was lying at her feet.

Wait, no. There was a man-shaped shadow far down on the opposite corner, only visible because when he moved his head it eclipsed one of the lights of the village.

So far away? Why was the monastery so lightly guarded?

That made her nervous.

Together her and her team crawled along the catwalk to a staircase leading down. This brought them into even greater shadow. They paused as a distant figure walked between buildings further down the slope. Once they heard a door slam, they made their way toward the big building they presumed was a temple, crouching low and hoping not to attract notice.

They got to the corner of the building and saw a pair of giant double doors on the front. Too much noise going through those, plus they were plainly visible to the rest of the monastery. Without a word they crept around and found a side door.

Jana gripped her MP5, peering into the night as Bledshaw took another lookout position, Jacob covered the door, and Aaron eased it open.

Dim candlelight shone from the corridor within. They hurried through and closed the door behind them, fearful of being spotted by someone outside.

Once inside, they paused and looked down the corridor. Doors stood closed to either side, and a door ten feet ahead of them was also closed. Beneath it shone light. They caught a faint whiff of incense.

They crept down to the end of the corridor, keeping an eye on both side doors. While they didn't like leaving unexplored areas behind them, they had to get in, grab some intel in the form of prisoners or plans, and get the hell out.

Aaron eased open the door a crack and peeked through, Jana looking over her shoulder. Bledshaw was right behind and Jacob, uncharacteristically, took up the rear. Did he not trust having Bledshaw behind him?

No time to think about the complexities of their group. They had a mission to accomplish.

It was a Buddhist temple. They looked upon a ten-foot-tall stone statue of the Buddha surrounded by statues of what Jana recognized as Tibetan demons, scowling figures with protruding tongues and fangs, wielding swords and enemies' heads. The back wall was painted with scenes of paradise and hell, mostly hell. All this was garishly lit by four flickering braziers set at each corner of the room. The smell of incense hung heavy in the air.

Nice décor.

They crept in, seeing no one.

Just then, a monk in a black robe trimmed with red came around the other side of the statue carrying a bowl of burning incense.

He spotted them in an instant.

With a loud cry, he dropped the bowl of incense and leapt a good ten feet, straight at her father.

CHAPTER TWENTY FOUR

Jana didn't dare fire. They were relying on stealth, and the monk's shout might not have been heard outside this building.

A shot sure would be.

Her father must have thought the same thing because instead of trying to fire, he brought up his AR-15 to block.

It didn't work. The monk kicked the assault rifle so hard it slammed into her father's face and he fell to the cold stone floor.

Jana leaped forward and swung the butt of her MP5 at the monk's head. He ducked and punched her in the ribs, doubling her over.

Bledshaw proved more effective. He landed a kick in the monk's chest that elicited a grunt and made the monk perform a backflip. He kept doing backflips until he got to the other end of the room and grabbed a sword hanging on the wall.

Uh-oh.

Jana surmounted the pain in her ribs, raised herself up, and aimed. The time for stealth had passed.

Too late, he was already on them, having crossed the room in the blink of an eye.

Jana only just managed to parry a blow that wound have cleaved her skull in two and got saved from the backhand by Bledshaw slamming the butt of his gun into the monk's head.

The blow was so hard it should have given the guy a concussion. Instead, it only made him duck to the right and circle in again for another attack. He kept close so no one could fire without the risk of hitting someone else on the team.

Another swing. Jana ducked back, and the tip of the blade missed her face by less than an inch.

Her father moved in and swept his AR-15 in an arc to take out his feet. The monk sprang up in the air, tucking his legs in.

When he landed a moment later, Jana was ready for him. She slammed the butt of her weapon into his face.

The monk staggered, stunned. Jacob dove in and sank a Bowie knife between his ribs.

Remarkably, the monk still managed to raise his sword over his head, tip down, ready to skewer Jacob. Jana swung at the last moment and deflected the descending blade.

Jacob wrenched his Bowie knife free and scurried back an instant before the sword swung in a deadly arc, catching only air.

Jana hit him again, making him stagger, then Bledshaw slammed him a good one and he fell to his knees.

Even down, he managed a swing that nearly lopped Aaron's leg off as he moved in for the kill.

The monk shouted something in Nepali, swung his sword to keep them at bay, and tried to stand. His robes were now soaked with blood.

He fell back to his knees. His eyes rolled up in his sockets and he fell over, dead.

"Damn, I hope the rest of them aren't that tough," Jacob muttered.

"I hope his shouting didn't alert the others," Bradshaw said, running around to the other side of the statue. Jana hurried back to the door through which the same. Readying her MP5, she peeked through it. The hallway remained quiet, the other two doors closed.

She returned just as Bradshaw did.

"No other monks and no other exits," the director of the Antiquities Division said.

Jana looked around. The temple in the other monastery was connected to the other buildings by a tunnel. It seemed strange that this one wouldn't be. But the side of the temple through which they entered stood apart from the cliff face. Those two rooms they had yet to explore wouldn't have a tunnel unless the entrance was in the floor.

She'd need to check, but first she remembered that an outcropping in the irregular cliff actually touched the back of this building, just about where the Buddha sat flanked by statues of demons. Jana edged behind the plinth and peered at the stonework, garishly painted with scenes of a flaming land populated by tortured souls and triumphant demons.

And then she saw it, a faint outline on the back wall, a seam barely visible within the colorful artwork.

She moved over to it and began to probe with her fingers. The surface felt like wood, not stone, but was so cleverly painted that even this close she couldn't tell the difference.

"What do you have?" Bledshaw asked, moving over.

"There's a door here."

Jacob and Aaron hurried over.

After more feeling around, Jana pushed on a painting of a giant pot in which several people were being cooked over an open fire, and there was a loud click. The wall shifted like a door, and a narrow portal swung open.

A dark passage lay beyond. They lit the mini flashlights strapped below the barrels of their weapons and peered inside. A roughly hewn arched passageway curved around and angled down.

Jana took point. There was only room for one person to go at a time, and she ignored Jacob's attempts to squeeze around her.

Staring down the barrel of her submachinegun, Jana paced down the sloping and curving corridor. After about ten yards, she estimated she had done a 180 and was now facing toward the slope and the rest of the monastery. This was confirmed by the fact that the passageway straightened out and sloped down at a more acute angle. Jana had to step carefully not to slip on the stone floor that had been worn smooth by generations of feet.

The tunnel ended in a large cellar. In one corner was a stack of steel cases like oversized suitcases. A short flight of steps cut into one wall led up to a closed door.

"These look like crates to hold drones," Jacob whispered.

While Jana covered the door, the men opened several of the cases. As they suspected, they held drones.

"Not finding any ammo," Aaron said.

"Maybe it's stored elsewhere," Bledshaw suggested.

Jana glanced at the ground. Only a small part of the floor near the stairs and the tunnel entrance had any dust.

"This room used to be nearly full of containers," she said. "Probably that fleet of drones they sent at us."

Her father nodded and came up to her, hopping onto the stairs in front of her.

"Ladies first," Jana said.

"You're not a lady, you're my little girl," he said with a grin.

Jana smiled and shook her head. Now wasn't the time to be cute, no matter how endearing it was. She and her father finally had a real relationship, and the world wouldn't let them enjoy it.

Aaron moved up to the stairs with the rest of the team just behind, listened at the door, and then opened it a crack.

They found themselves in a workshop. On a large table sat two partially dismantled drones. A side table held a large toolbox and various electronic parts next to a rack of tools along one wall.

Unlike the cellar and tunnel, this room was lit. Aaron pointed to a soldering iron on the worktable that was still on.

Jana tiptoed to the door on the opposite wall and listened. She heard footsteps coming closer.

Raising a finger to her lips, she indicated the door and got ready to strike.

The men moved to help her, but before they could make it, the door opened.

The monk barely had time to register surprise before Jana knocked him unconscious with the butt of the weapon.

A quick glance into the next room, which was a second electronics workshop, indicated the monk was alone. Bledshaw dragged him inside and zip tied his wrists and ankles.

They headed into the next room, where they saw a detailed topo map of the region around the Monastery of the Sacred Lotus.

"There," Jacob said, pointing. "I bet these three red dots are where they set up the drone operation bases. See how all three points have a clear line of sight to the monastery but are far enough away not to be spotted by the human eye?"

"Interesting," Bradshaw said. "But I'm a little more concerned about what they're planning on doing rather than what they already did."

"Wiseass."

They moved to the next door and came to a hallway with three doors along one wall and one at the far end that Jana judged to be the outside door from what she remembered of the dimensions of this building from when she saw it on the catwalk. Light shone from beneath all three doors on the left. From the nearest, they heard the static of a radio.

Jacob inclined his head toward that door. Jana nodded. They needed to take out any external communication first. The force that had attacked the monastery might still be out there getting ready to cause more mischief.

They flung open the door to see a small room with an expensive shortwave transmitter on a desk. The monk manning the radio spun around. Jacob went to club him and got a fist in the gut instead. Jana smacked him, and the monk fell to his knees. Jana swung again, but the monk grabbed her gun, twisted it out of her grasp, and aimed it at her.

Suddenly, Jana had her own gun barrel pointing right at her eye.

A shot rang out. Jana jerked back. The monk clutched his chest and sank to the floor.

Aaron had fired right between them to hit the monk straight through the heart.

"Damn," her father muttered.

They rushed into the hallway just in time to see the other two doors fly open and a monk look out of each. Bledshaw shot the first one but the other slammed the door shut in time to avoid the same fate.

Bledshaw rushed down the corridor, kicked the door open, and fired. The rest of them hurried to follow. Jana glanced in the side room and saw only the man Bradshaw had killed and a collection of maps.

When she got to the room where the second monk had retreated, she saw a couple of computers with Nepali text on the screen and an open window. They could hear the monk screaming for help from somewhere in the shadows.

Not that there was any need call for help. All that firing would carry through the clear mountain air like an air raid siren.

Jana ran to the door at the end of the hall, opened it a crack, and saw it opened to the outside with no one in sight. About ten yards away stood another building. It was silent, its windows shuttered.

"I think—"

Before she could finish her sentence, a figure dropped down from the roof and kicked her full in the chest. She flew backwards and landed hard on the ground.

Her head smacked against the floor, and she blacked out.

CHAPTER TWENTY FIVE

One thing Jacob Snow had noticed right from the start of his active service was how time seemed to go more slowly in a firefight. From the moment Jana got kicked by that monk and he gunned the bastard down, to the point where they were surrounded with monks coming in at them from all sides probably hadn't been more than five minutes.

It felt like years.

The small ops center they defended was completely surrounded and the main problem was that with Jana still unconscious, they didn't have enough people to cover all the entry points. Thc building had a door and three windows, plus the tunnel from the temple. They were three people trying to cover five entry points.

And the monks were coming through all five of them.

But they weren't just throwing knives and shuriken—one of which had already grazed his shoulder—but also firing AK-47s and throwing smoke grenades.

Jacob coughed and blinked as he peeked out the window of the map room, which while exposing him to enemy fire gave him a lovely breeze of pure air, and aimed his Russian-made RMG. Some of the monks were sniping from the windows of the next building down the slope, trying to keep Jacob and his companions' head down while the monks snuck up and tried to jump inside. That had almost worked twice already, and he was sure they'd try again. They kept having to run from room to room to check, exposing themselves in the hallway to fire from the doorways on either end of the corridor. It was pure luck; none of them had been killed yet.

That and skill.

His skill served him well as the RMG round hit the wall just between the two windows from which monks were sniping. The bunker buster round blasted a fist-sized hole through the stone wall before the second charge denotated. Both windows lit up with the blast and a double plume of smoke issued from them.

That's one less problem.

The next problem came in the form of a monk leaping through the window with the ease of a little girl playing hopscotch, except he had a pair of knives in his grip. No little girls Jacob had ever met accessorized like that.

Jacob only had his grenade launcher in his hands and backpedaled madly, blocking a flurry of blows. A shot from Aaron took him out, but Jacob had just backed all the way into the hallway and got grazed by a knife thrown from one of the doorways at either end. A line of pain seared across his back.

He leapt back into the map room. They had crossfire from the hallway now and were trapped in the three rooms. They were losing control of the situation. A dozen monks lay dead or dying, but they just seemed to keep coming.

Jana still lay unconscious. Jacob had tucked her under the map room table. Out of the line of fire, at least for the moment.

"You guys all right?" Jacob shouted, dropping the RMG and pulling out his MP5.

"Yeah," Aaron said from the radio room.

"Yes," Bradshaw said from the computer room. "We seem to be in a bit of a pickle."

"That's putting it mildly."

"We—" a burst of fire drowned out Bledshaw's words. "If we keep getting rushed from the windows like this, sooner or later they'll get bold enough to come down the hallway at the same time."

"Don't give them ideas!"

"They're perfectly capable of thinking of this them—" another burst of fire drowned out the Antiquities Division director.

God, that guy's annoying. Damn good fighter, though.

Jana moaned and stirred. Jacob squatted down.

"You OK?"

"Ugh. What happened?"

Another monk flew through the window, but instead of carrying a pair of knives, he carried a pair of pistols. Jacob gave him a burst from his MP5. The monk jerked and both guns went off, hitting the floor to either side of Jacob. The monk's limp body slammed into him. Jacob rolled with the impact and threw him off.

They ended up near the door, when all of a sudden a blast pushed him back.

Oh crap, they're using grenades now.

Jacob blinked, coughed, spat out a mouthful of grit, and struggled to rise. The combination of getting knocked to the floor by a dead body and then knocked to the other side of the room by a grenade blast had taken it out of him.

Just as he got to his feet, he saw a second grenade fly across his field of vision along the corridor.

He threw himself down to cover Jana. The grenade detonated, sounding like it landed at the far end of the corridor.

Through the pounding in his ears, he heard Tamang's voice.

"The corridor is clear. Come on out and let's get going!"

They emerged from their rooms, Bledshaw having to turn back and shoot at someone.

"I thought I told you to guard our escape route!" Aaron shouted.

"I am your escape route," Tamang said.

Aaron turned to Jacob and grinned. "I like this guy. Where did you get him?"

"Rent-an-Agent. I'll pick up Jana and let's go."

He turned back to the room to see Jana on her feet, gathering up maps and books.

"This isn't the time to catch up on reading."

"I'm gathering intel."

"Good point."

Tamang rushed in. "I've cleared a path through the tunnel to the temple, but we don't have much time. They'll close in again."

"Here," Jana said, dumping some paperwork on him.

"I only have one arm! How can I shoot?"

"This is what we came for. I'll explain later."

Tamang looked at one of the papers. "Whoa! It sure is. How could you tell?"

"I looked at the pictures."

Jacob shook his head in wonder. She had only just regained consciousness, and she was already analyzing ancient manuscripts.

The group hurried down the corridor back in the direction of the workshops. Half a dozen dead monks lay in their path.

"I'm going to have to start calling you the one-armed bandit," Jacob told Tamang.

They got into the cellar and then the tunnel with no further trouble and ran down its length. Jacob worried that the monks would appear ahead or behind them and open up with their Kalashnikovs. In this confined space, there would be no way for them to miss.

They got to the turn and ascended carefully, peeking around the edge of the inside wall. Other than a couple of new dead bodies, there was no one.

“Not bad for only having one hand,” Aaron said.

“I got them from behind,” Tamang said. “They weren’t expecting me.”

“That may be true, but you’re being modest, my friend. Getting the drop on these guys is a hell of an accomplishment.”

They got to the temple and out. They paused for a moment for Jana to catch her breath. She was still rattled from getting knocked out.

Spotting a robe hanging on a peg behind the altar, she grabbed it and bundled it around the precious maps, papers, and books she’d found. Tamang dumped his own load into the robe.

"Let's go," she gasped, nearly at the end of her strength. Jacob looked at her with concern before realizing the rest of them weren't any better off. The cut from his knife wound made his back sing with pain, and he could feel blood trickling down his back.

No time to deal with that now. The monks would regroup and be on them soon.

They checked the door, were surprised the coast was clear, and hurried out, keeping an eye on the roof. The monks had a bad habit of dropping from roofs or popping out of the most unlikely places.

To Jacob’s shock, they got all the way up to the parapet and down the rope ladder on the other side without encountering the enemy. They hurried out into the darkness, desperate to find shelter where they could hide out the night and plan their next move.

CHAPTER TWENTY SIX

Jana sat by a crackling hearth and puzzled over the documents Tamang translated for her.

It had been an exhausting, nightmarish retreat through rough mountain passes buffeted by frigid winds. They moved almost blind, not daring to light their flashlights and having to rely on meager starlight to guide them.

At last, they made it back to her father's camp, but they did not stop there. Instead, they continued down the slope another mile to a Sherpa's cabin occasionally used by herders. A stout little stone structure, it had a good supply of firewood, which they gratefully piled into the hearth.

No one would see the light of the fire with all the shutters firmly closed. Jacob and Bledshaw both needed it badly. Their coats had been cut in the monastery fight, and they were shivering and on the verge of frostbite.

Now Aaron was out in the night keeping guard while Jacob and Bledshaw patched their wounds and their coats. By the light of the fire, Tamang and Jana went through the papers they had found.

She had come to one conclusion right off.

"I'm thinking most of the monks left after they sent that numeric code over the air," she panted. "That place was big. Why did only a few dozen come at us and not hundreds? And we saw none of the Anglos Jacob spotted through his telescope."

Tamang nodded. "It makes sense. They would have been able to get back after the attack on the Monastery of the Sacred Lotus. They're quick and know all the shortcuts. Plus, the military didn't spot any of them remaining in the area. But perhaps they didn't come back here. Perhaps they went to a rendezvous with the bulk of the people who had remained in the monastery. They're obviously planning some big operation. The question is—what and where?"

Jana gestured at the heap of maps and papers and old volumes she'd plundered.

"Hopefully the answer is in here."

They got back to work, Jana looking for significant images, Tamang translating, both of them trying to puzzle out unlabeled marks on several maps.

It was a long, meticulous project neither of them really had the energy for. She had held up in the excitement and cold of the retreat, but now that they were in a cozy cabin with their sleeping bags tempting them, their eyelids grew heavy and they had to struggle to stay awake.

The maps seemed to indicate troop movements and attacks, but strangely in two widely different locations. One showed activity on the outskirts of Kathmandu. The other showed activity not far to the north of their position, on the Chinese side of the border.

"Do the monks have the manpower to conduct two different operations?" Jana wondered aloud.

"Depends on the type of operations," Tamang replied.

"Good point. Maybe these papers will give us a clue."

The old books were hard to interpret. They were written in an old form of Tibetan, and while Tamang spoke Tibetan as well as Nepali, it was like a modern reader trying to read Chaucer. He had to read out loud, slowly enunciating each word to get its meaning and still having to guess at some of them.

They had no time for that. At least they got the gist of the books, which was on the power of the *car mey* and how the Royal Vajra could activate them. The activation process was all but unintelligible, a combination of prayers, religious references, and some form of mediation neither of them had ever heard of.

The books offered many distractions—long religious lectures, parables, and discussions of fine points of philosophy. The pictures were even stranger, with everything from demons to monks using magical powers to a temple made out of ice.

They also contained numerous references to the *cyar mey* being used not only as a power source, but also as a weapon of war.

Tamang snapped his fingers.

"If they have the Royal Vajra and can use it like the abbot used the one at the monastery, they could cause an electromagnetic pulse to short out Kathmandu's power supply! Everyone will think the Chinese are behind it."

"Come on, they'd need some sort of mechanism for that, like the one hidden in the Buddha statue. That would be huge, at least the size of a truck."

Jana was guessing about that. She was no electrical engineer, and neither was anyone else in the group. There had to have been something inside that Buddha statue, although she had no idea what it would look like or how it would function.

"Who says they don't have one waiting there?" Jacob said from his spot at the hearth.

"Another step towards World War Three," Bledshaw said.

"I don't think they need anything besides the Royal Vajra," Tamang murmured.

Jana looked at him curiously. There had to be a mechanism of some sort. He knew that.

She decided they didn't have time to debate it.

"Let's get into these papers," she said.

Those proved even more difficult than the old volumes. While not exactly in code, they had been written in a deliberately vague manner. The monks who needed to read these texts already knew the main gist and needed only to look at them for reference. That made them hard to figure out for outsiders.

Tamang and Jana worked deep into the night, long after Jacob and Bledshaw had curled themselves up in their sleeping bags and drifted off. Aaron remained outside on a lonely vigil.

Jana found herself wondering about him. He had spent so many years doing what he was doing tonight. He deserved a long break, perhaps a break for life.

But the world wouldn't let him. The world wouldn't let her, either.

She focused on the papers.

At long last, they figured out their meaning, or at least as much of their meaning as they could.

There would only be one attack, with the monks concentrating their entire force and their unnamed allies to make a definitive strike. They would use the Royal Vajra to ignite the *cyar mey* to deal some sort of blow at the target. While the most obvious attack would be some sort of electromagnetic pulse, the papers seemed to hint at something more than that.

There had been a discussion between which of two proposed targets would be best. Obviously, they meant Kathmandu and this region in Tibet. One was decided upon, but the papers make no mention of which.

"Time to get the rest of the team in on this," Jana said. "We've learned as much as we can."

Tamang shook Jacob and Bledshaw, who snapped awake instantly like the trained fighters they were, while Jana walked out into the night. The chill air revived her somewhat, although she still felt like she could curl up on the nearest patch of ice and sleep for twelve hours.

She let out a low whistle, three different tones that was a code she'd used with her father since she was eight.

The return signal came. A few seconds later, he appeared.

"We've figured it out. Sort of. Come on inside."

They gathered around the maps and discussed what she and Tamang had worked out.

"So the question is, if they're only going for one target, which one will they go for?" Jana said once they were done explaining everything.

Tamang tapped the map of Kathmandu. "I know the main power station for the capital and surrounding region is right about here where these markings are. And over here … " he pulled out the map of Tibet, you can see several gorges perfect for hydroelectric plants. The Chinese have several in this region and major relay stations scattered around. They power all of Tibet. I have no idea if these markings relate to the stations, though. Neither of these maps has any manmade features on it, just the natural topography."

Jacob rubbed his jaw. "Any electromagnetic pulse that shorted out a regional power supply would be seen as an act of war."

"Big time," Aaron agreed. "So which to go for? All the attacks so far have been on Nepal—the theft of the Royal Vajra, the attack on the border guards, the attack on the monastery. So it makes sense to hit Kathmandu. It fits the pattern."

"Two out of three of your examples don't count," Bledshaw said. "The theft at the museum was necessary in order to bring forward the plan. The attack on the monastery was to stop us from interfering. Only the attack on the border guards was truly intended as an attack on the Nepalese state, and one event does not make a pattern."

"He's got a point," Jacob said in rare agreement. "So we have to ask what the goal is here. If the attack is on Kathmandu, the Indian army might move in to ensure its own national security, setting off a diplomatic nightmare. If the attack is on China, then China might move into Nepal."

"If the target is China, then why not attack the Chinese border guards?" Aaron pointed out.

"Border fights happen sometimes," Jana said. "People get jumpy, a shot goes off, and things snowball. Diplomats on both sides are usually eager to smooth things over. Taking out a whole region's power grid is on a whole other level."

"That still doesn't answer the question of why they didn't attack the Chinese side of the border to ratchet up tensions before taking out the Chinese power grid and starting away."

Jana shrugged. "Tension got ratcheted up anyway, and with the monks coming from Nepal, it's easier to strike the Nepalese border guards. That border post was clear on the other side of the country. Plus, the Nepalese soldiers aren't as well trained and equipped as the Chinese troops. No offense, Tamang."

"None taken. They are stronger than us, which is the problem. And the Indians will use it as an excuse to come on into our country."

Jana blinked. He had never called Nepal his country before.

Jana went on.

"I'm thinking we should go after them into China and try to cut them off. We can warn the Nepalese to be on their guard, and they'll listen to us. I'm not sure we can convince the Chinese of anything at this point. Dad, you told me how they got super paranoid because of the hydroelectric dam attacks, even though they weren't on their own soil. Now, they must be doubly paranoid because of all this instability in Nepal. While I'm not convinced the target is Tibet, we have to pick one to go after and if we're wrong, the Nepalese government has a chance to stop them. I say we go to China."

Aaron chuckled. "Go to China. While I agree with your tactical assessment, I don't think going to China will be as easy as all that. All the passes will be guarded on both sides of the border."

"True. But we got to find a way."

"Follow the monks," Bledshaw suggested.

Jana turned to him. "I beg your pardon?"

He shrugged. "Follow the monks. They'll go to one of the passes and take out the guards on both sides. Then they'll leave radio operators at both bases to call in, saying everything is fine while the rest of the force continues to the target. If we follow the monks' route, we'll only have to deal with those detachments."

Everyone looked at each other. Jacob spoke first.

"There are a lot of assumptions in that statement, but we've been running on assumptions this entire mission. I say we try and figure out the route they took and follow them."

Jana wondered if those were really all assumptions, or if Bledshaw knew something he wasn't sharing.

Bledshaw smiled. "I'm glad you're gaining some confidence in me. Does this mean you'll reconsider my offer to join the Antiquities Division?"

"Don't push your luck."

Tamang studied the map. "Time is of the essence for them so I think they will take the most direct route, which would lead them through this pass. It's a small one and out of the way, so it probably doesn't have very big garrisons. If we take this valley here, we can cut off some time and catch up to them a bit. Let's use the satellite phone to warn the Nepalese government. They can put the base on alert and maybe send some reinforcements. I'll try to convince them the threat is real and not from the Chinese."

"All right," Jana agreed. "The battle at the monastery must have surely attracted the attention of the village down in the valley. They'll call the authorities. That will add credence to your report. Maybe the garrison can stop the monks."

Tamang made a face. "No. They'll get slaughtered. But maybe they can slow them down enough for us to catch up."

CHAPTER TWENTY SEVEN

The Nepalese garrison did not slow the monks down enough, and neither did the Chinese garrison. Jacob knew that the instant he found the bodies.

He and Aaron crept along through a rocky pass, darting from cover to cover, approaching the rear area of the Nepalese base. Just as they came in sight of the bunkers, they spotted a heap of bodies dumped in a ravine.

All wore the uniform of the Nepalese Armed Forces.

They continued past empty bunkers and beneath abandoned lookout points until they got to the HQ, a squat concrete structure sunk into the bedrock. A radio mast stood on the roof. They checked the door. Unlocked.

They entered, then winced as the door gave out a loud creak.

The main room had a table with topographic maps and a rack of guns. A couple of open doors led into other rooms. From one came a monk, asking a question as he rounded the corner.

Just as his face registered surprise, Jacob and Aaron threw knives that plunged into his chest.

He gasped and fell to the floor, coughing up blood.

Even before he choked out his last, Jacob and Aaron had cleared the bunker, found four bodies of monks under a tarp in one of the rooms, saw no one else was inside, and met back in the main room.

"You go get the others. I'll neutralize the radio operator in the Chinese bunker," Aaron told him.

"I didn't see any maps or anything here."

"There won't be. They know where they're going. Thankfully with all these mountains in the way they can't get a signal from the monastery. Even the jump on a shortwave skip will go past them, not to them. They won't know about the attack on the monastery."

"Which means the survivors we left to our rear will be coming after us."

Aaron punched him in the shoulder. "All the more reason to hustle. See you soon."

Jacob hurried back to where Jana, Bledshaw, and Tamang sat hidden behind some boulders. Bledshaw was watching the trail behind them with a pair of binoculars. Jana and Tamang were poring over one of the old books.

"See anything?" Jacob asked the director of the Antiquities Division.

"Nothing. Are the two bunkers cleared?"

"One is. They only left a single man. So Aaron will clear out the other one by himself. Let's go."

"We've found out something else," Jana said, holding up the book. "At least we might have."

"What?" Jacob asked, giving the pass behind them a nervous look.

"A reference to the *cyar mey* having to be activated at certain sacred spaces. This book mentions a temple of ice somewhere in this region. There's even a picture of it. See?"

Jacob looked at a crude woodcut of what looked like a glacier in the shape of a pagoda.

"You can't make a building out of ice. Ice shifts with its own weight and changes in temperature. Even glaciers move."

"I know. But perhaps it's a metaphor. Perhaps there's an old monastery around somewhere that they're going to set up base in."

"Does the book mention where?"

"Not exactly."

"Does it mention if there are other monasteries around?"

"No, but this book is four hundred years old. There have been lots of monasteries built since then all over the Himalayas, especially in Tibet. We're going to have to look for an old one near the strike point."

"Good thing to keep in mind. Let's go."

They headed out. Jacob hoped they weren't too far behind the monks and whoever was helping them. Jana said that abbot had revved up the vajra in the Sacred Lotus monastery in just a few moments. It probably wouldn't take long for the monks to set up whatever it was they had planned.

They might have set it off already. They might be walking straight into an advancing Chinese army, intent on invading Nepal.

***

It was midafternoon and everyone was getting exhausted. He and Bledshaw had only gotten four hours sleep. Jana and Tamang had gotten half that. Everyone trudged slowly along a snowbound trail. They were several miles into Tibet now and had to keep to the back trails, half-guessed from the topographic maps, to avoid Chinese patrols. They knew they were on the right path, however, because of the footprints in the snow.

Jacob guessed them to represent almost sixty people, most wearing the smaller, local boots of the Nepalese, and the rest the larger, Western-brand boots of their foreign assistants.

Dr. Harlow? The Order? Both? They still weren't sure.

Whoever they were, they needed to be neutralized.

At least the prints were relatively fresh. They weren't too far ahead. And they had the Royal Vajra with them. Every now and then there was a large rectangular imprint in the snow like they had set down a crate or platform they were carrying it on.

The trail passed through a canyon and opened up to skirt the edge of a mountain. Far below ran a raging river that frothed and stormed through a narrow gorge. A hydroelectric dam blocked it and they could see a relay station and heavy power lines passing down the gorge and out of sight.

They stopped and consulted the topo map. The gorge they were seeing continued for a few miles before meeting with two others with their own rivers to form a large river continuing to the lowlands, or at least what passed for lowlands on the Tibetan plateau.

"I think they'll hit the power supply at this meeting point of the rivers," Jacob said. "That's where the markings are and that's where there will be the biggest relay station. The Chinese probably have dams all along these three valleys and then a big one where they meet."

"Makes sense," Jana said. "Let's go."

Another few miles of slogging along proved him right.

After passing a couple of more dams in the gorge, the view to their north opened up and they saw two more gorges meet the one they had been following. Just beyond their juncture stood a huge dam. From this ran a massive network of power cables running off down the valley.

"Impressive," Jacob said.

Jana gasped and pointed. "Not as impressive as that."

He turned to where she indicated and gasped too.

On the upper slopes of the mountain stood a single large stone temple of ancient design tucked under an overhang of rock. It shone bright in the sun and made Jacob squint even though he wore trekking glasses. It looked almost as if it was made of the sun itself.

"Why is it … oh, it's covered in ice!" Jacob cried.

"The temple of ice," Tamang gasped. "Just like in the ancient text."

Bledshaw pointed. "Look at that channel right above it. It must thaw out on warm summer days sometimes and turn into a stream that covers the roof and walls with water that ends up freezing."

"That's where we need to go," Jana said. "That's where they'll set up the Royal Vajra. It has a clear view of the entire electrical network."

Suddenly, they remembered their situation and got out of sight behind a boulder.

"We'll have to ascend the mountain, get above the temple, and then come at it from above," Aaron said.

Jacob groaned inwardly. It looked like a long, hard climb, and while they had crampons to put on their boots and ice axes, they had no other climbing equipment.

But they had no choice. The monks, while they thought they were alone and undetected, would still guard the main approach to the temple. The only chance was to come around behind them, exhausted as they were.

Jacob looked around at his team, at all the drawn faces and bloodshot eyes, and saw no one who wasn't ready.

"Let's do it."

CHAPTER TWENTY EIGHT

Jana had never been afraid of heights before, but then again, she had never tried to climb down an icy channel on a thirty-degree slope down to an overhang that dropped off sheer. One false move and she'd end up sliding down, striking the temple's arched roof, and sliding right off to plummet to the hard stone below.

She inched down the slope, digging in with her crampons and her ice axe, her legs scissoring from fatigue. The others inched along next to her.

They were making too much noise. With every step, they had to dig into the ice to keep from slipping, and that sound must have carried far in the clear air.

She hoped the updraft of wind that had frozen her face was carrying the sound away from the monastery.

At least she hadn't seen any guards. The monks and their foreign helpers must have decided that no one would be foolish enough to try and approach the temple from above.

Why do I have to prove them wrong? I'm going to break my neck!

Jana wondered what would happen when the firing started. Would it set off an avalanche? There was nothing but a sheet of ice above the temple, so perhaps not. Or would that break free to come crashing down on all of them?

She was more worried about crashing down on the temple herself. She decided to worry about a possible avalanche later.

"Maybe we should just use the RPGs to blast the temple from above," her father said through gritted teeth. He was having trouble with this descent, too, and that was saying something.

"No," Jana, Bledshaw, and Tamang all said in unison.

"It's priceless evidence of Civilization X," Bledshaw said.

"It's Nepal's most sacred object," Tamang said.

Jana said nothing more. Her father's suggestion was a good tactical decision, and yet she couldn't bring herself to agree. She wasn't sure why she didn't want the thing destroyed. It was a sacred object, true, but she was more concerned with stopping a war breaking out. Surely that took priority. But there was something else to the object, something with significance beyond geopolitics. That ethereal glow of the vajra in the monastery … the electromagnetic pulse … the way the abbot's wounds seemed to have vanished …

… something else was going on here. Something profound.

Her foot slipping and Jacob grabbing her reminded her to focus on the present.

"Thanks."

"Almost there."

"And then what?"

"We go down the left side. The slope isn't as bad over there. On the right side it's steeper."

What Jacob didn't mention, but Jana had certainly noticed, was that on the right side just past the front of the monastery it sheared off to a vertical cliff a couple of hundred feet high. One wrong move, and they'd plummet to their deaths.

"Left side sounds like a good idea."

They continued their exhausting and slow descent, pausing a moment when they heard chanting carried up by the wind.

"The monks have started the ritual," Tamang said. "We need to get down there now."

"What are they saying?" Jana asked.

"It's Old Tibetan, I think. Older even than those books we puzzled through. I can't understand it. Remember what the texts said. Activating the Royal Vajra takes a full ritual, not like the one in the monastery. It's far more powerful."

"We need to hurry," Jana said, picking up the pace. "That ritual might not last long."

Just then, the ice cracked under the foot she had put her weight on, and she fell flat on her back. Hands reached for her, but it was too late. She shot down the icy slope like she was on a playground slide. She scrabbled with her feet and tried to get her ice axe dug in.

All those efforts did was slow her down a bit, so when she landed hard on her rear end right next to the temple, she didn't break her tailbone.

It sure felt like it, though.

Before she could rise, a European-looking man carrying an AK-47 ran around the corner of the temple. He stopped, stared in shock for half a second, and raised his gun.

That half-second of hesitation was his downfall. Jana threw her ice axe, and it hit him square in the face. He fell backwards with a grunt.

Jana sprang up and rushed him. The chanting inside the temple continued, and maybe if she could take him out quietly, they could keep the element of surprise.

The guy wasn't dead. He was clutching his bloody face with one hand and trying to get up with the other.

Just as he opened his mouth to shout, Jana kicked him.

She still had on her crampons, and the effect on his head was devastating.

Jana paused over the bloody ruin of the guard, gorge rising in her throat. The chanting continued. She shuddered, readied her MP5, and peeked around the corner.

She was in luck. The temple had a portico at the front that meant that the sentry had been standing out of sight of the front door and whoever was standing on the other side of the portico. Her embarrassing fall and its bloody aftermath had gone unnoticed.

The rest of the team joined her. They took off their crampons to move more silently on the snow-covered platform and headed around the corner.

They were just getting to the corner of the portico. Her father and Jacob pulled out grenades. Jana raised a cautionary hand. They didn't know how close to the entrance the Royal Vajra might be.

Jana was just about to take a peek when two monks came around the corner, both armed with swords.

They let out a shout. Tamang fired a burst from his M4 that took them both out.

No more time for stealth. They rushed around the corner only to come face to face a line of monks and foreigners standing inside the colonnaded portico just in front of an open doorway leading inside the spacious interior of the temple.

Aaron and Jacob tossed their grenades, and everyone ducked back around the corner as the enemy line opened up. Jana cried out as she felt a bullet graze her shoulder.

Then they were out of the line of fire. The two grenades detonated.

They leaped back around the corner to find the entire line down. Beyond was the doorway, and at the far end of the interior was an altar on which the Roya Vajra rested. Already, it was glowing with a dim golden light.

Monks sat in four rows in front of it. An older monk stood in front of the Royal Vajra with his hands raised. They had been chanting but now leaped up, drew swords and other weapons, and charged.

The older monk, who Jana took to be the abbot of the Monastery of the Invisible Lotus, didn't budge.

"Fire low so you don't hit the Royal Vajra!" Tamang shouted, dropping to one knee and opening up with his M4.

The rest followed suit, including Jana.

The monks began to fall, but they rushed in, dodging and leaping, making it harder to hit them. With five trained agents firing assault rifles and submachineguns, they should have mowed them all down before the monks got anywhere near the door.

Instead, a quarter of them made it.

And then it became a fight for their lives.

Swords came slashing down, spears jabbed at their faces, and fists and legs tried to beat them into the ground.

Jana shot down one monk, only to get slammed to the ground by another. A foot came right for her throat, threatening to crush her windpipe, when a shot from one of her companions knocked the monk fly to the side. Jana rolled out of the way of a spear aimed at her gut, shot the spearman, and sprang to her feet.

The old abbot still stood at the altar, and the Royal Vajra was beginning to pulse, its golden glow getting brighter.

She ran for the altar. A monk leapt at her from her left, sword held high, and she shot him in midair. Then she turned, and as she suspected, three monks were right behind her. Flicking her gun to full auto, she mowed them down.

Jana sprinted across the room. Just as she got to the altar, the abbot turned. The glow of the Royal Vajra began to dim.

The old monk clenched his fists, and the callouses on them were bigger than Jana's knuckles.

She aimed and fired.

Only to hear the click of an empty magazine.

Uh-oh.

The old monk rushed her. She tossed her gun at him and went for her pistol.

Too late. The abbot batted away the heavy gun like a fly and landed a punch to her midsection that made her feel like her stomach had been wrapped around her spine.

She felt herself getting lifted into the air and tossed aside like a rag doll.

Luckily, she fell on the dead body of a monk. If she had fallen on the hard stone floor, she would have been knocked unconscious or worse. Even so, she lay stunned and helpless as the abbot rushed for her.

Jana fumbled for her pistol, painfully aware that she wasn't going to get it out of the holster in time.

So she fired it anyway.

The bullet burned her clothing and creased her thigh. The abbot jerked and stumbled, blood spurting out of his ankle. He balanced on one foot and looked ready to spring at her.

Jana yanked the pistol from its holster and put a bullet between his eyes.

When she turned to check on her friends, she found them finishing off the last of the monks.

For a moment, there was silence in the room except for the low hum of the Royal Vajra, and then that, too faded away. No more light came from the sacred object.

Jana struggled to her feet, every part of her body aching. The rest of them all had wounds too.

A groan from the portico. Remarkably, one of the foreigners who had been hit with a grenade was still alive. He moaned again, and tried to roll over, but his body, covered in wounds, couldn't manage it.

Jana moved over to him, feeling a mixture of rage and pity. Rage for his taking part in trying to start a war, pity for the man's terrible state.

His eyes opened, he saw her, and he moved his jaw.

No!

Before she could stop him, he bit down on something that made a soft cracking sound and he immediately began to twitch.

The smell of almonds rose from him.

Cyanide. The Order always took cyanide to avoid falling into the hands of the authorities.

Bradshaw walked up to her side.

"What a foolish thing to do," he muttered.

Then he turned and looked more closely at one of the other dead foreigners.

"I know this man. He worked in the Antiquities Division as a researcher for our East Asian bureau. He was supposed to have died in a climbing accident."

"So we have proof now," Jacob said, looking at Aaron and Jana.

Yes. Proof that the Order and Dr. Harlow are working together. Great.

Which means we're up against a far deadlier enemy than we ever faced before.

And it means we've only won the opening round in a long, long fight.

Suddenly Bledshaw pointed at the altar.

"The Royal Vajra! It's glowing again!"

Everyone turned to look. Jana stared, confused. It wasn't glowing at all.

"Drop your weapons and raise your hands above your head, please," Bradshaw said.

Jana groaned. All this time, he'd been lying in wait to steal the artifact from under their noses. All that helpful advice, all that fighting by their side, it had all just been a means to an end.

"You bastard," Jana muttered.

She put down her gun and carefully withdrew her pistol and put that down too.

The others followed suit. Then they turned to look at Bledshaw.

He had his M4 pointing right at them.

CHAPTER TWENTY NINE

While Bledshaw's gun did not waver, Jana noticed something strange in his face.

What was that? Indecision? Fear? The corners of his mouth twitched, his eyes grew wide, and his gaze flicked all over.

Then his gun did begin to shake.

Maybe I can get to my gun, Jana thought.

She edged a few inches toward it. Bledshaw's gun jerked toward him.

"Stay where you are!"

"Or what? You're going to gun me down and call in your buddies from the Antiquities Division to take the Roya Vajra? You'd not only be betraying us; you'd be betraying your nation. Or does the Antiquities Division no longer consider itself a branch of the United States government?"

Bledshaw winced. His breathing came fast, and not just from the recent exertion and the altitude.

For a long moment, they all stood there, facing each other in silence. Jana remembered his knife was still in its sheath. She decided to throw it. While Bledshaw would blow her away the instant she drew, it would give the others a chance to do something.

Then Bledshaw's look of indecision was replaced by one of calm resolution.

Oh, crap.

Bledshaw smiled. He put his submachinegun on the floor and patted it.

"The Curator made me swear to take the Royal Vajra from you. I think this counts as keeping my word. I tried, you see, but my gun has slipped from my fingers."

"That's a hell of a stunt you pulled," Jana said. "I was about to throw my knife at you."

"I was too," Aaron said, "until I saw you weren't serious. I could see in your eyes you wouldn't shoot."

Bledshaw hung his head. "I intended to, at first."

Aaron walked over and put a hand on his shoulder. "You only thought you did. The better part of your nature came through."

"So is the Antiquities Division on their way?" Jana asked.

"Not unless I give them a signal with a special compact satellite phone. Sadly, I think I will accidentally drop it off a cliff. I really do have butter fingers."

Jana walked over to him. "Why didn't you follow orders?"

Bledshaw grimaced. "I kept thinking about what the abbot said to me. Remember what he said? 'If you clean out the pig's stall with your hands, you cannot complain of sickness when you bite your nails.' A bit obscure, to be sure, at least to all of you. But I've been cleaning out the Curator's proverbial pig shit for years and it's been making me increasingly uneasy and nervous. So biting my nails would make me sick. Spiritually sick. I'm done. I cannot quit. One does not quit the Antiquities Division, at least not easily, but you can now consider me your friendly neighborhood double agent."

He gave a dramatic bow.

Jana smiled, then looked at the Royal Vajra.

"He told me that true education expands constantly. I think I know what he meant by that."

Tamang stepped forward. "He told me that I would die on this mission. I think I have, in a way. While I was always proud of my heritage, I never believed in the religion. Not really. Seeing what I've seen these past few days has changed my mind."

Jana looked to Jacob, who looked at the floor and said nothing. The abbot had told him, 'do not be ashamed to be a reluctant warrior, for that is the only good warrior there is.'

She knew he wanted to quit. Even though he never spoke the words, she knew him well enough to know that.

Jana went up to him, held both his hands, and kissed him. Then she whispered in his ear,

"The abbot was right about you too."

Jacob smiled and squeezed her hand.

***

A secret base outside Pyongyang, North Korea
The next day

“Stopped again,” Dr. Colin Harlow growled. “The same damn team has stopped me again.”

"I told you that you shouldn't have canceled my hit," Goran Hribar said.

"Quiet, Agent Twelve. I told you we couldn't find their hiding place soon enough, and we had to move up the schedule for the Royal Vajra operation because of the museum opening. Damn! Why did the royal family have to make such a momentous announcement at the last minute?”

The pair sat in a dreary concrete ops room loaned to them by the North Korean government in exchange for some sensitive military technology and the promise of more to come. Dr. Harlow had bribed many corrupt governments, but none had been cheaper and harder to deal with than the North Koreans.

At least they were out of reach here.

The third man in the room spoke up. He was unusually tall, a shoo-in for the NBA if he hadn’t been so thin and obviously unhealthy. He had a sickly gray pallor and coughed regularly into a handkerchief spotted with blood. His eyes, however, held a feverish intensity.

He was the representative for The Order, and neither Harlow nor Hribar knew his name.

“Our contact in the CIA cannot uncover their safehouses quickly enough before the targets move to another one.”

The demolitions expert raised his hands in frustration. “Then how the hell am I supposed to take him out?”

“Now that we know they will come out of hiding any time there’s a crisis, we just need to make another crisis,” the representative from The Order said.

“As long as it doesn’t delay our schedule,” Dr. Harlow said.

“It won’t. In fact, it might speed it up. Your ancient artifacts are a most intriguing source of power, and The Order is very pleased to make this collaboration with you.”

Harlow wasn’t pleased. He didn’t trust the man or the organization he represented. Not one little bit.

But he needed their resources. His own had taken a big hit with the failure of the last operation.

“So what do you have in mind?” he asked.

“An operation that will be sure to bring out Agents Snow and Peters, their daughter, and I’m sure Mr. Bledshaw too.”

Harlow nodded. “That would be good.”

"And the way I have this operation set up it will bring them all to a precise spot at a precise time and that's when you, Mr. Hribar, will have the chance to show off your expertise in explosives."

"Tell us the plan," Hribar said, interested now.

The representative of The Order explained it, going through every detail. As he did so, the demolitions expert and Dr. Harlow smiled.

And those smiles kept getting bigger.

NOW AVAILABLE!

TARGET TEN
(The Spy Game—Book #10)

“Thriller writing at its best... A gripping story that's hard to put down.”
--Midwest Book Review, Diane Donovan (re *Any Means Necessary*)

From #1 bestselling and USA Today bestselling author Jack Mars, author of the critically acclaimed *Luke Stone* and *Agent Zero* series (with over 5,000 five-star reviews), comes an explosive new action-packed espionage series that takes readers on a wild ride across Europe, America, and the world—perfect for fans of Dan Brown, Daniel Silva and Jack Carr.

In the shadow of the fallen Byzantine Empire, CIA Agent Jacob Snow and his daring archaeologist partner Jana discover a deadly quest for the last treasure of the Romans. As they traverse the perilous terrain of a Turkish island, they face a high-stakes puzzle only they can solve—but will the cost be higher than they bargained for?

An unputdownable action thriller with heart-pounding suspense and unforeseen twists, TARGET TEN is the tenth novel in an exhilarating new series by a #1 bestselling author that will make you fall in love with a brand-new action hero—and keep you turning pages late into the night.

Future books in the series will soon be available.

“One of the best thrillers I have read this year. The plot is intelligent and will keep you hooked from the beginning. The author did a superb job creating a set of characters who are fully developed and very much enjoyable. I can hardly wait for the sequel.”
--Books and Movie Reviews, Roberto Mattos (re Any Means Necessary)

Jack Mars

Jack Mars is the USA Today bestselling author of the LUKE STONE thriller series, which includes seven books. He is also the author of the new FORGING OF LUKE STONE prequel series, comprising six books; of the AGENT ZERO spy thriller series, comprising twelve books; of the TROY STARK thriller series, comprising seven books; of the SPY GAME thriller series, comprising ten books; of the JAKE MERCER thriller series, comprising five books (and counting); and of the new TYLER WOLF thriller series, comprising five books (and counting).

Jack loves to hear from you, so please feel free to visit www.Jackmarsauthor.com to join the email list, receive a free book, receive free giveaways, connect on Facebook and Twitter, and stay in touch!

BOOKS BY JACK MARS

TYLER WOLF THRILLER SERIES
DOUBLE AGENT (Book #1)
DOUBLE CROSS (Book #2)
DOUBLE ASSET (Book #3)
DOUBLE DOCTRINE (Book #4)
DOUBLE JEOPARDY (Book #5)

JAKE MERCER THRILLER SERIES
ABSOLUTE THREAT (Book #1)
ABSOLUTE DAMAGE (Book #2)
ABSOLUTE FORCE (Book #3)
ABSOLUTE PERIL (Book #4)
ABSOLUTE TREASON (Book #5)

THE SPY GAME
TARGET ONE (Book #1)
TARGET TWO (Book #2)
TARGET THREE (Book #3)
TARGET FOUR (Book #4)
TARGET FIVE (Book #5)
TARGET SIX (Book #6)
TARGET SEVEN (Book #7)
TARGET EIGHT (Book #8)
TARGET NINE (Book #9)
TARGET TEN (Book #10)

TROY STARK THRILLER SERIES
ROGUE FORCE (Book #1)
ROGUE COMMAND (Book #2)
ROGUE TARGET (Book #3)
ROGUE MISSION (Book #4)
ROGUE SHOT (Book #5)
ROGUE STRIKE (Book #6)
ROGUE ORDER (Book #7)

LUKE STONE THRILLER SERIES

ANY MEANS NECESSARY (Book #1)
OATH OF OFFICE (Book #2)
SITUATION ROOM (Book #3)
OPPOSE ANY FOE (Book #4)
PRESIDENT ELECT (Book #5)
OUR SACRED HONOR (Book #6)
HOUSE DIVIDED (Book #7)

FORGING OF LUKE STONE PREQUEL SERIES

PRIMARY TARGET (Book #1)
PRIMARY COMMAND (Book #2)
PRIMARY THREAT (Book #3)
PRIMARY GLORY (Book #4)
PRIMARY VALOR (Book #5)
PRIMARY DUTY (Book #6)

AN AGENT ZERO SPY THRILLER SERIES

AGENT ZERO (Book #1)
TARGET ZERO (Book #2)
HUNTING ZERO (Book #3)
TRAPPING ZERO (Book #4)
FILE ZERO (Book #5)
RECALL ZERO (Book #6)
ASSASSIN ZERO (Book #7)
DECOY ZERO (Book #8)
CHASING ZERO (Book #9)
VENGEANCE ZERO (Book #10)
ZERO ZERO (Book #11)
ABSOLUTE ZERO (Book #12)

Made in the USA
Columbia, SC
26 September 2024